something like ideal

something like ideal
brent stephen smith

Natalie! life be filled with
May your excite and
adventure best,
All the
Brent x

ISBN 978-0-9810752-0-4

Questions and comments related to this work can be addressed
to the author at brentstephensmith@gmail.com

All business-related inquiries may be directed towards the
author's representative at jonas.eli.cohen@gmail.com

for all the other travelers
-bss

prologue

You've left your boy then, have you? Sad thing, that. Was he good to you? Did he make you smile? A shame, shame. I don't think you understand what kinds of pain that can cause. Oh, sure, they look all tough, them, but God, every man has his softness. It'd surprise you, I'm sure, to know that he'll be missing you, long after you've moved on.

It's funny I should run into you here. I'd just arrived in town, and came for a small drink and low and behold, here you were, having a stiff one, letting out to the barkeep about your former boy. I didn't mean to interrupt, but old Mic, there, he don't mind.

I know I look a little rugged, and to be fair, the road and rail have been well-traveled, twice over, at least. You still have a bit of a twinkle to you, girl, even if it's a bit sad today, yeah. Not a day older, do you look, it's true. Yeah, I know I look a bit rough, but you know that I get a little red when I drink, too. Just a few so far, but I'll stick around if you're wanting to chat. It's been a long time. Too long.

I've just been running along, moving from here to there, trying to fill the gaps, so to speak. I'm still searching for that something. You know, you remember, I mentioned it a long time back, that something.

Well, it ain't perfect, and I'm not sure if it's meant to be, but I think I've found it. Not me, no, I haven't been so fortunate. But, damn, I've seen it. It's out there, it seems. I have to be a bit more optimistic, I suppose. Seeing you here might be a sign, God knows. Another pint of the dark, Mic, thanks. Yeah, seeing you, it's weird. I'm not sure of what to make of it, so I'll just spill my guts, let out this whole story. You can stick around for that, yeah? It's been too long, you can't go. Mic, something for the lady, too.

1.
the train station

Daibhead stood on the platform as the train pulled away and tried to compose himself enough to wave. His weak arm flailed in the wind as the four-car train disappeared beneath the horizon. He had long known that this day would come, but that provided scant relief to a boy who had just said goodbye to his girl. Summer had crept up quicker than he had imagined until it was too late; Ánna was gone.

Now what to do with his time? They had spent the last four years side-by-each on numerous teenage adventures; skipping stones across the shallow tide pools, playing tag with kelp, day trips into the city to sneak a pint where no one knew them, or curling up under a blanket out in the fields and staring upwards at the shooting stars. All of these things were lost to Daibhead. Even when Ánna returns things will be different. She had left the village as a girl to volunteer in some remote corner of the earth and would only return at the end of the summer as a woman. The enormity of it all encompassed Daibhead as he walked from the station back to home.

He took a meandering route through side alleyways and across park greens, crossing from the town centre at the footbridge to the more residential southern part of the village he lived in, walking along the river path until he met the main road which he traversed to reach the public house.

As he entered the doorway of the pub the sympathetic faces of Marla, the barmaid, and Alan, the barkeep, greeted him. Daibhead's father was nowhere to be seen.

"Hullo Daibhead, is she off then?"
"She is."

Marla wiped the counter down with a leisurely pace and met Daibhead's eyes directly.

"Gonna be alright?"

"I'll try, t'anks Marla."

Alan was washing pint glasses, placing them upside down to dry with a pace to rival Marla.

"Have ya got any plans for yer summer?"

"I haven't."

Alan took a second from his washing to look at Daibhead. The boy's face was worn. He could tell that beneath the skin Daibhead was hurting. A quiet trembling, you know?

"Perhaps some reckless behaviour: heavy drinkin', drug usage, gamblin', yeh?"

"Yer a funny man, Alan."

"T'anks, I try my best."

Daibhead nodded as he glanced lazily from side to side.

"Is my Da 'round?"

"I t'ink he's gone ta city for supplies. Won't be back 'til supper time, 'magine."

"'Kay, I'm jus' gonna head upstairs."

"See ya later then, Daibhead."

Daibhead went up the back stairway to the living quarters, grabbed a newspaper from the table and retreated to his bedroom. On the walls were various pictures of Ánna and him. Daibhead fixed his eyes on one beside his bed, sitting on the nightstand, staring until his eyes became red with irritation and he began to cry.

*   *   *

The driver almost fell backwards when he lifted up the large suitcase to place in the cab for his attractive young client. He had expected it to weigh substantially more than it did. Anticipating a heavy load he lifted with nearly all of his strength and in return found himself flying back with all the grace of a slapstick comedian.

"It empty, ma'am?"

He looked earnestly at the woman, hoping for some answer that would alleviate his embarrassment.

"No, I should think not. But it's not filled with bricks or mortar, either."

He frowned and meekly lifted her large assortment of smaller baggage into the cab. His only consolation was that perhaps having witnessed his humiliation the woman would provide a decent tip.

*   *   *

Daibhead smiled as his watery eyes opened to the sight of his grandfather bringing in a cup of tea and placing it at his bedside.

"T'anks."
"Not a problem, lad, yer sure ta be missin'er."

Pádraig Shannon gave a warm smile to his grandson and left him to drink in peace, taking the newspaper. He walked down the hall to his own room where he had already set his own cup and saucer, with a few biscuits on the side, on the nightstand. The elderly man undressed from his well-worn sweater and soft tweed pants and changed into the crisp striped pajamas he had laid out on the foot of the bed. Crawling into the bed he propped up a couple of pillows against the headboard and began to drink his slightly cooled tea. Across his lap sat today's *Independent*, the distinctive green harp calling back at him from some distant space. Paddy nibbled on his biscuits, alternating with sips of tea, as he worked his way through the news.

*   *   *

Alan swept behind the bar, whistling some old forgotten tune, diligently keeping up to task with the chore list his boss had left behind. Marla stared vacantly out the window at the sleepy main road. It was late afternoon, perhaps half-three, and the pub's employees were expecting the post-work crowd to start trickling in at any time. On a Friday like this, in mid-May, with the weather approving, a pleasant after work pint could turn into a two a.m. walk home. The public house was just that, a gathering place for the public, a home for the villagers to congregate, drink, laugh, and catch up on the latest gossip. Just before four, after a couple older gents had already taken up residence at a corner table, Daniél Doyle walked in.

"Jus'in time, Danny; almost four."

"Yeah, I'll agree to that, half the town's heading up the road, nipping at my heels to get here."

"Lucky for ya, I'll be helpin' ya serve that lot."

"You'll be looking for a fair tip, I imagine, too."

"Half'yers are prolly mine on any given night anyways, ya jus' happen ta swoop in at the right moment."

"Having a sense of charm can't hurt either, hey, Alan?"

"Funny, Danny, funny."

Just as he had suggested, following Danny in, came a large crowd of customers. At the front of the pack was a tall, lanky, awkward looking man with an unlit cigarette dangling from his mouth, every bit a rake. To his side was a rather fat bloke who seemed to be laughing at the lanky man's every movement.

"...And so I says, I says: 'listen'ere, ya old fuck, ya owe me two hundred, and I don't see it next week, I'ma kick yer ass.'"

At this point the lanky man mimed punting a ball from his hands.

"'Jus' like that', I says."

"And didya Fintan? Didya?"

"I sure as hell didn't, ya know why?"

"Why?"

"Cuz he ran straight to the bank an' came back with a handful'f cash."

"No!"

"He did."

"Right away-like?"

"Yeh, right away."

"All two hundred?"

"N'a penny short."

"Fantastic!"

"Well, lemme tell ya, Sorley, that he passed on the word that ya don't owe me money."

"I bet."

"Owe Fintan Larkin money an' he'll kick yer ass righ'ta the bank."

"Right on Fin."

"I've settled up with four others since. They got the message, Sorley, they got it, alright."

"Bang! Wallop! Kablammee!"

"Exactly, my fat friend, exactly."

Danny looked at the friends and could only chuckle to himself about how odd a pair they appeared. He had known Fintan and Sorley since he was a child; he had even had the displeasure of being beaten up by Fintan in the park green over a misunderstanding. Of course, that was many years ago, Danny had been eleven and Fintan sixteen; since then they had both grown up and it was all water under the footbridge.

"What can I getchya, Fin?"

"Have a pint of plain and my fat 'ssociate will have somethin' light, he's on a diet."

"Shut it, I'll have a stout, too."

"Is that part of your regimen, Sorley?"

"Yer both a bunch of wisearses."

"So, stout is it?"

"Ya, an' that's enough from ya. Don't expect a large tip."

"I never do. You always manage to pay in exact change."

"Mother taught me ta be wise with money, Doyle, and I ain't gonna waste it on the likes'f you."

"Funny, Sorley, yer mother didn't teach y'anything 'bout investing. A treadmill would've paid some major dividends by now."

Having to fill their glasses, Danny left Sorley to be further tormented by Fintan.

"Hey Sorley, have you heard 'bout the second footbridge they're plannin'?"

"No, wha's the story?"

"Well, I've heard they're gonna sneak up b'hind ya one day, roll ya ta the river, an' walk 'cross yer fat shoulders ta th'other side."

"Very clever. Pokin' fun a' the fat guy, again."

"If ya struggle an' start wigglin' yer legs they figure they might be able ta generate some hydroelectricity."

Fintan exploded with laughter at this point, unable to resist his own jokes. Sorley sat and smoldered for a few seconds while he planned his rebuttal.

"Well ya know Fintan; I've heard that they have some plans fer ya too."

"An' what're those?"

"They figure they can rub yer two spin'ly arms t'gether an' start a fire."

"That wa be pretty impressive, ya'd have t'admit."

"I guess so, I jus' thought'f that one now."

"Cou' be 'Fintan the Fire-man'. Women would line up, 'round the street corner, jus' ta get the chance ta warm up next me."

"Hey Marla! Wouldya ever line up for the chance ta warm up next Fintan?"

The barmaid put down the glass she was pouring, looked straight at the two eager patrons, walked to their end of the counter, put both hands on the edge of the counter and leaned forward, inches from Fintan's face.

"This, right now, is as close as'will ever, an' I mean ever, wannabe, ta disgustin' twig like you, Fintan Larkin."

The entire bar within earshot laughed hysterically. Fintan was only mildly embarrassed and his face hid it well.

"Tha's alright, Marla, y'ain't m' type anyways."

Marla let that one go and returned to pouring the glass. The customer who had to wait for his half-filled pint only gave her a larger tip.

*   *   *

When he heard the rapping at the front door, Daibhead rose quickly and ran to answer. What greeted him there was a complete surprise.

"Sara!"

"Hello Daibhead, how are you?"

"Not bad. What're ya doin' here?"

"I've come back to town for a bit. Spur of the moment thing. I hadn't even thought about a place to stay."

"Shouldn't be a problem. M' da's out, but he oughtta be back soon, I'm sure he won't mind. Come in."

"You're a sweet boy, Daibhead Shannon."

"T'anks, Sara, but I'm not a kid no more. I've even finished school, for now, anyways. I might go ta uni, but I haven't really figured any 'f that out yet. No matter really, I'm eighteen; plenty'f time ta figure these t'ings out. 'Magine yer quite hungry. Can I getchya somet'in' ta drink?"

"Slow down; let's start by lugging in my luggage."

"Wow! Those are a lotta bags you got."

"Well, I have been moving from place to place. That's my entire life you're looking at."

"Ya must've had a lot of livin' in the last two years! Didn't y'only leave with one small bag?"

"Ah, that's what makes you a man: you just can't see it like a woman would. In my bags I have more clothes, because, unlike here, where it only rains or has spurts of mild sun, I've gone to places where the weather changes. I've had to adapt."

"I was under th'impression that there were only four seasons; ya seem t'ave packed fer sixteen."

"I guess I am looking for more. Winter is not the same thing as severe winter, Daibhead, not even close."

"Well, le'see'f we can find a place in a corner somewhere for ya ta store the fifteen seasons'f clothes ya won't need while yer here."

16

*   *   *

Danny stared down from the counter at the two men wrestling on the ground.

"Hey! Sorley O'Mara will you quit kissin' Fintan and knock it off?"

The aggressor looked up at his accuser and snarled.

"Fuck off, Doyle, I ain't kissin'm, I'm kickin' his arse."

"Sorley, Fintan; get up now."

The two recognised that voice.

"Yer both welcome ta waste as much money as ya want on pints here, bu' this ain't no fight club."

"Sorry Eoghan."

"Sam'ere."

Fintan Larkin and Sorley O'Mara were dumb, but they weren't dumb enough to pick a fight with the pub's owner. They reset themselves atop their favoured stools and ordered another round.

"No more fightin'?"

"None."

"Danny, two pints'f ale fer our friends, here."

*   *   *

"Tell me, Saraid, what brings ya back?"

"Well, Pádraig, it just felt like the time to come back and reconnect with everyone for a bit."

"You've been lotsa places."

"There'll always be some roots in me, though. You haven't got rid of me for good."

The old man slapped his knee as he chuckled at the thought. It wasn't often that he had the pleasure of such company. Saraid Doran was extremely attractive, a real beor, and, had Paddy been about fifty years younger, well within his tastes.

"What was yer favourite city?"

"Hmmm, Barcelona. No, wait, Berlin, no, it's all a toss-up. They were all amazing."

"Excellent, my dear, excellent."

Sara looked at Paddy and thought he had aged twenty years since she left. Two years ago, he had still been busy serving pints downstairs at this hour of the night.

"You look older."

"True 'nuff. I feel older."

"If it wasn't for your familiar blue eyes I wouldn't be able to pick you out of a crowd."

"I'm sure ya'd be able, I'd be th'only old man who wouldn't be starin' gawk-eyed back at ya."

"You're still a pretty good flirt for your age, Paddy."

"I'd say I'm pretty terrible, I'm wastin' all this good stuff on a hopeless case like you. Though, ta be fair, most women my age don't need too much encouragement. I've also got th'advantage 'f'being wunna the few gentlemen 'round that still has his teeth."

"For your age, that is."

"No, jus' in general. Have ya seen summa th'ugly fellas downstairs?"

"Well, they can't all be ugly, now, can they?"

"Are y'askin' 'bout a specific someone?"

"Are you going to make me embarrass myself?"

"I t'ink ya'll find Daniél Doyle is tendin' bar tonight."

"Goodnight, Pádraig, I'll talk to you in the morning."

She kissed the old man's cheek and left him to his nightcap and the muted sports highlights on the television. Sara opened the door that led to the stairway down into the bar, took a deep breath, exhaled, and walked down into the dimly lit establishment.

2.
another pint, please

"Cheers, ta Sara's return home!"

Eoghan led the crowd in raising a glass to the young visitor.

"Cheers!"

The whole room drank the moment in. Those that knew her drank in her honour, raising fists high, the mugs and glasses spilling onto the floor and patrons, singing songs of homecoming, and laughing at themselves as they entertained Sara.

The older men took their turns to come and meekly say 'hello' to Sara, tipping their caps and moving along after bumbling a few words. Any girl from Leinster was a looker in their eyes, but Saraid Doran blew them all away with her casual air of sophistication. She was well-bred, well-educated, and well-traveled and the average man at the pub lacked any and all of those qualities. The younger men also lacked some of the wisdom of their seniors and almost immediately began fawning over her, as if she were any other girl on a Friday night, oblivious of the fact that her eyes kept focused on the man behind the bar.

"Hello Danny."

Now, don't let the veneer fool you, they'd warn; he's as clever as they come, that Danny Doyle. An abandoned mill, on a dried-up creek, he'd come to life with the flow of a torrent through him when *she* returned. When he came to life again they could see his elegant grace around them all, glowingly pouring out of him, what with every step he took and every word that traipsed across his tongue. Everyone knew men like he, a rarity, the men that seemingly could part the waves if so they pleased and yet knew not the power within their hands. And, if they did come to life, how the embers would burn in their eyes, intensely smoldering, but not in anger, just the kind of benevolent passion that every woman aches for, yet seems destined to lose for some lesser light; for burning suns are often too hot to hold. That was Danny Doyle.

"Hi Saraid."

Danny barely made eye contact as he continued to mix drinks. Sara watched him anxiously, waiting to say what she had been wishing to say for almost two years.

"Busy at work, yeh?"

Her casual question betrayed her thoughts. Danny spoke as if her question was the only thing on her mind. He knew better, but, were she to be coy, he'd play that game.

"Trying to keep on top of things. How're you?"
"Well, thank you. It's good to be back."

Sara meant every word. It had been a long time since she had seen Daniél Doyle and he had changed, but only for the better, she could see. Two years ago he had been absent-minded and foolish. He had given up on the two most promising things in his life: university and her. Sara could tell that Danny had spent some time thinking about both and he wore a maturity that she instantly found appealing.

"Is it? How long do you plan on staying?"
"A while."
"Well, then I guess we'll run into each other then."
"I'd like that."

*　　*　　*

"I haven't been able to do anything lately."

Mícheál Farrell looked at the desperate face of his brother. Nicolás was the sort of artistic type that wore his emotions openly and yet still managed to confuse any onlookers. You know the sort, the kind that were so honest that their honesty was mistaken for an act. He didn't have a drop of pretense in his blood, but if you didn't know him, you'd say he carries that disaffected air of an artist that rubs some the wrong way.

"Nothing. Not one drop of paint to canvas in over a month."

"That's too bad, Nic. I hadn't noticed this change in you."

"And I shouldn't have expected it, no, don't be sorry."

Nic knew better than to expect his brother to notice these sorts of things. He had always found Mícheál to be less than observant. Growing up they had often fought over misunderstandings that cut Nicolás deeply and barely bothered the distant Mícheál.

"Well, what's causing this, this, drought?"

"Inspiration, Mícheál; I'm lacking it."

"Well, I don't know what to say, I'm not exactly the artsy type."

When he was a child Mícheál had once painted a landscape scene, just to prove a point to Nic that there was nothing to it, and that it was just a waste of his time. In a fit of rage, Nic tore the painting up. Now in their late twenties, both men had come to a somewhat comfortable understanding of the other.

"I've got something inside me that needs to come out, but I haven't been able to even think of it, let alone express it."

"Are you a queer, then?"

"No, Mícheál, I'm not gay."

"Sorry, not even funny, I realise that."

"How do you manage to do what you do?"

"I'm a butcher. Not a whole lot of dry spells for me. Don't need any real inspiration. People like meat."

Being the town butcher was not Mícheál Farrell's first choice occupation. He had gone to architectural school and had dreamt of moving to Glasgow to pursue a career designing high-rise residential buildings. In his last semester, his father, Mickey Farrell, Sr., passed away suddenly of a brain hemorrhage. In order to support his mother, and avoid a pending foreclosure on the Farrell home, he dropped everything and returned to run his late father's butcher shop.

"I meant how do you manage to be who you are without worrying if you are going about it all wrong?"

Years ago that sort of question would have dug deeply at Mícheál. He knew that he had an obligation to take care of his mother and that the butcher shop was the sure way of doing it. He knew that Nicolás appreciated his self-sacrifice; it was Mícheál who had helped pay for Nic's art classes. What kept him going was the thought that he could always go back and finish that one semester. Glasgow was not going anywhere.

"Listen Nicolás, I've seen your paintings. I know what you are capable of. You're better at that than anything else. Stick with it. I don't know what to do about your dry spell but I do know that it isn't a sign that you ought to be doing something else."

*   *   *

Monday afternoons were always quiet. Danny enjoyed them as there were often only a few patrons in the pub. Those days were so quiet that Eoghan only scheduled one person to work.

Usually that meant Danny.

"A pint, please."
"Hullo, Maks."

Across the bar sat Maksim, the grocer's son. His father, Sergei, rarely came to the pub, though it was only across the street, but Maksim enjoyed dropping in occasionally on his way back from the train station.

"How are ya, Danny?"
"Not bad. Enjoying the sun today?"
"It's a good day out there alright."

The warm May sun was beaming in through the windows. The only thing that Danny disliked about that was that it made all the bar's imperfections readily apparent. It also highlighted the dirt and grime that Alan had missed cleaning Sunday morning. Because Mondays were so slow it usually meant Danny had to duplicate Alan's chores.

"How are your studies going?"
"Coming along now. Been reading a lot of history lately."
"Good on ya. That's my old speciality."
"Is it true you left the university after your second year?"
"It is."
"Why was that?"
"I dunno. Felt like it was a waste of my time."

Daniél had lacked any focus at that point in his life and making claims of wasted time was like pouring water into the ocean.

"Did you not enjoy any of it? Any of the subjects?"

"I did. I liked history. I just wasn't keen on being forced to read something rather than read it for the sake of enjoying it."

"What's your favourite time in history?"

"Probably the early twentieth. Wars, depression, independence."

"Revolutions."

"Exactly."

"I can't stand the revolutions."

"No? Why's that?"

"All that suffering, fighting, for what?"

He stared intently at the older bartender as if waiting for some dispatch of truth to be relayed.

"For change."

Maksim's face soured.

"Change? What changed?"

Danny was surprised with that response. He had always taken it as self-evident that revolutions brought about change.

"People felt as if they were controlling their own destiny, Maksim; that's what changed."

"A load of shit, that. Nothing changed."

"Do you not think that fighting back against the English to win our freedom was a change?"

"Win your freedom. I'm not Irish."

In the midst of the discussion he had forgot that the Abramovs had not always lived in town.

"Okay, do you not think that fighting against the Czar was a change?"

"It only brought in more controlling powers. Communism was a sham. We weren't brothers; there were privileged people as always."

"What about overthrowing communism? Was that not a revolution?"

"That's even worse, it's real, it's not history, I know that one. There's no change. My cousins don't control their destiny any more now than my uncles did theirs. The oligarchs control everything and the only thing that we have now is a sham vote for a president who runs unopposed."

"Does that not call for a new revolution?"

"No. It's just more bloodshed, more anger; none of that is worth it."

"What is worth fighting for?"

"Nothing. I can't think of anything that is worth fighting for. Violence only creates more violence. It has never brought any good."

"What about defeating oppressors and freeing enslaved people? Tell me those aren't worth fighting for?"

"Fine, I will give you those. But, let someone else do the fighting. Not me."

"That's quite a take on things."

In the short young man across from him, Danny saw a darker, more cynical version of himself.

"I don't see the point of me fighting. I have little chance of being the difference maker. I'm not a large man, nor am I a strong man. I am better off with my books, buried away with the Babylonians. There are thousands of others who could easily fill my place on the frontline."

Danny agreed with most everything that Maks said. As always, he pushed the conversation.

"Not even if Mother Russia called on you?"

"I owe her nothing. She's abused my family for centuries and we're now alien. I owe her no more than I owe Zambia or Argentina."

"Do you not feel any sense of identity?"

"None."

"You speak Russian with your family, do you not?"

"I do."

"And yet, you feel nothing?"

"Nothing."

"That's a sad case, Maks."

Danny felt the same thing. He had no idea what made him who he was. At least Maksim had a piece of home in his family, his culture, and his language that linked him back. Danny remembered about a dozen words in Gaelic, things his grandmother used to yell at him when he spent summers with her in Galway.

"Danny, you as sure as anyone ought to know the dangers of nationalism. How can you try to tug at me with these calls to 'Mother Russia' when you know what evil nations have caused? Wars fought in the name of the national cause. Fuck that. Genocide committed in the names of nations. Fuck that. Bombs destroying one nation so that another nation can feel muscular and proud. *Fuck that*. My identity is in who I am, regardless of where I come from. Fuck nationalism."

"Those are all valid points. I don't disagree that extreme cases of nationalism have caused unspeakable horrors. But, I also think that there have been positive cases of national pride. Do you watch the Olympics? I love them. I could care less about track and field but every four years I am cheering on every Tom or Colleen. I don't think that's too bad, now is it?"

"Thanks, Danny. I do like the Olympics. Can I have another pint, please?"

3.
one night out

It's funny, you being here, and all. I never thought I'd find you like this. Here I am telling tales, stories, and you just sit there and listen. Don't go nowhere, please. I'll share a little more with you, because the drink has loosened my tongue. Let me sing summat:

I don't know where all this goes
I'm lost
And so are you

I don't know where all this goes
I'm lost
And so are you

So far away
So very far
I almost forgot your face

So far away
So very far
I almost forgot your face

Don't come back now
I've got nowhere to take you

Don't come back now
I've got nowhere to take you

It took me so long
To realise
I'm not what you're looking for

And if you come back
You'll find me
Somewhere on the street
Begging for a piece of meat

Begging for some change
Change
We could both use some change
I don't blame you Molly

*   *   *

Daibhead sat along the river's path, throwing sticks into the murky greenish water. One by one, the stray sticks would disappear with the slow-moving current until there were no sticks left to throw from where he sat. He got up to collect some more, but, once up, abandoned his plans and began to walk down the path, in the opposite direction the sticks and the river flowed, in the opposite direction of his home.

He walked without any sense of urgency and seemed to just float westward. His eyes felt glazed over as if he hadn't blinked in some time. The trees above and in front of him appeared as brown and green smears. The river just sat beside him as a deep murky green stripe in his peripheral vision. He walked.

*   *   *

"Well, ya bastard, it's fair time we head out for a night and leave this sorry pub."

Fintan snarled at Sorley. Four pints in and he had decided tonight was as good as any to cross the river into the town centre and test the small, but lively, nightlife.

"Yer lucky I'm in a dancin' mood, Fin."

"Ya lookin' ta dance with me?"

"No, but I t'ink I'll have a few moves on the dance floor that will reel in all the women."

"Sorley, when I hear the word 'reel' I t'ink'f Ahab pullin' in yer fat white ass."

"Funny."

Sorley didn't mind Fintan's jokes because he was in a jovial mood and quite willing to dance the night away with whatever lucky lady earns the honour. Fintan's attitude wasn't a traditional help for the purposes of being a wingman but it somehow helped to make Sorley appear more attractive by comparison.

"Another pint?"

Alan had seen their glasses empty in a hurry and had come to pre-emptively alleviate the situation before they began hurling insults his way for slow ale delivery.

"Sorry Alan. We're headin' out."
"It's early. What's going on?"

He had never seen the two patrons leave the pub before nine on a Saturday and was genuinely astounded.

"We're headin' 'cross the bridge fer some dancin'. Goin' ta meet us some proper ladies. Not a whole lot goin' on here."

Fintan scowled as he said the last sentence, nodding in the direction of Marla, who was finishing her shift. Alan had never thought that the two clowns would consider leaving. He had even made a deal with Danny that he would get the exclusive right to serve them that night, hoping for some accidental generosity in the way of tips the more the night wore on. Typically, Fintan and Sorley were quite meagre with their tips, but the more they drank the more liable they were to overspending. Alan had suggested to Danny that only one of them deals with the two so that the tips at the end of the night were well earned. He had often spent nights alternating serving with Danny only to have Danny receive the bulk of tips, whether out of chance or otherwise and had devised a way to ensure he would receive adequate remuneration for the hassle involved with the poison-tongued Fintan. Alan frowned as the two left.

*　　*　　*

Paddy sat in his bed, listening to the evening news over the radio. The Taoiseach was resigning. A good man with a troubled present. A real shame, Paddy thought, a real shame. His hands trembled as he sipped his tea. He had grown worse over the last few weeks, much to everyone's ignorance. It wasn't that they didn't notice him; it was more that they didn't see him. He rarely left the Shannon home, save for a quick visit to the grocery store across the street, or downstairs, into the pub he once owned. There were plenty of clues and everyone knew that he was not the same as he had been just a few years ago, back when he was filling pints and playing cards. He was a frail, helpless shell of the brash, broad man he used to be. But no one could tell the difference between the man of May and the man of April. That is, no one but Pádraig Shannon. It all seemed so very long ago, but his mind was still sharp and he knew the difference. The radio whispered the day's events as he fell asleep.

*　　*　　*

Under the stars, Daibhead walked with an effortless pace, propelled onwards by his youth. The kind of energy that cannot be replaced in later years pushed him to keep going. Reaching the next town from his own gave him a kind of satisfaction he had never experienced before. Daibhead felt as if he were on a mission, if only for himself.

As the walkway steered him along the foreign town's streets and shops he saw another world from his own. Every type of store he knew from his own town was right here, with a different name, different signs, and different people. Daibhead was as far from home as he could imagine. He crossed the river road and walked on the walkway beside the shops, gazing into the dimmed windows, grasping for a taste of this town's life; a life that was not his own.

He walked past the grocery store and thought of the Abramovs.

Did an immigrant family also run this grocery store? What was their story? What brought them here? Daibhead imagined a family walking from a distant land, following the river's path until they arrived in this very town.

A quaint, young family, with nothing on their backs but the clothes they wore. Dreaming of opening their own grocery store, they leave everything in their old life behind and follow the river. Daibhead turned around and began walking home.

*   *   *

"Sorley, yer an idiot."

"Shut it, Fin. I swear she's inta me."

"If she's inta you, then I'm the Pope."

"Well, yer Excellency, I'll be seeing y'at mass tomorrow mornin'."

Sorley left his friend to stew. Fintan wouldn't normally care at all about who Sorley was hooking up with, but tonight had been rather unsuccessful for himself and he realised he would be walking home alone. Fuck it, he thought, the fat tub could use a piece of luck.

*   *   *

"Thanks again, Marla, I really appreciate you coming out with me tonight."

"Not a problem, Saraid, I'd like t'unwind after a long week'f work."

"It's funny how to get over working in a bar all week leads you to coming out with me to another bar."

"Well, ta tell the truth, seein' other people havin' a good time makes me a bit jealous."

Sara looked at Marla and saw her for what she was. Beneath the smiling veneer was a sad girl waiting for something. Sara had been there. Sara was there. Sara knew. Sara was Marla and Marla was Sara.

"Can I ask you something Marlene?"

"Sure, go 'head."

"Does Danny ever talk about me? I mean *us*? Does he ever?"

Marla thought about it for a second. Recalling it was not a hard thing, but trying to say it right was. She wanted to say it right.

"He did, fer a while. After ya left, he talked 'bout ya non-stop. And, then he stopped. Hasn't said a word since."

It was exactly as she had feared; she had said it wrong.

"Oh."

"I'm sorry, that came out wrong. He occasionally mentions yer name. Mostly when he's talking' 'bout somet'in' in the past."

"Bad things?"

"No, no, no. I mean 'f'we're ever talkin' 'bout a movie or somet'in', he'll say somet'in' like 'oh yeh, I've seen that one, Saraid made me watch it.' T'ings like that."

Sara Doran smiled to herself. She *had* made Daniél Doyle watch an obscene number of awful movies and made no apologies about it. It was the kind of soft culture that a rough Connacht man like him needed. She smiled again to herself. He wasn't that rough.

"Thank you, Marla."

"I'm sorry for misspeakin'."

"It's alright."

A breeze passed through them as they walked to the town centre and relieved all the tension. Marla sighed and followed Sara into the club.

4.
all's well in may

Tressa Bradigan placed the teacup and saucer on the table for her waiting guest. Daibhead softly lifted the cup in his hands and took a small sip, testing to see how hot the tea was. His grandmother sat down across from him with her own cup and smiled kindly.

"So how're ya doing, dear?"

"Fine, Nan, jus' fine."

"Are ya missin' her yet?"

"I am, of course."

"How long has it been then?"

"I dunno, haven't kept track."

"Really?"

"Okay, it's been twelve days."

Daibhead exhaled, showing his frustration.

"So, what is she doin', then?"

"She's gone t'Africa. She's livin' in a small village. Volunteerin' at an orphanage."

"Well, that's lovely, now isn't it?"

"T'is. I'm prouda her."

"And you, dear Daibhead, what're yer plans fer summer?"

"I dunno. Probably help Da with the pub."

"That's quite the comparison, then: Ánna helpin' those children in Africa and you servin' pints ta these scoundrels, here."

"I haven't really got n'other options."

"Whaddya plan fer fall? University?"

"I dunno."

"That's okay, I am sure ya'll figure these t'ings out."

"Yeh."

*   *   *

"Paddy, come to supper!"

Paddy heard his mother's call and he ran to the farmhouse. When he arrived, his father had already begun eating the dark stew and was dipping his bread into it. His large hands tore the bread into smaller pieces that he would dip and then stuff into his mouth. There was still a piece in his mouth when he greeted his son.

"Sit down, Pádraig."

"Yessir."

"Had a busy day, today, then?"

"I have, sir. I took care'f Bridget jus' as y'asked. Been groomed."

"Didya clean out stalls?"

"I did."

"Good, good. Finola, sit down, 'ready. Let's eat our supper as family. Paddy, say grace."

Paddy looked at his father who had already been eating and then looked at his mother who meekly shook her head without Paddy's father noticing.

"Dear Father, we t'ank ya fer this bountiful meal that we're 'bout ta receive. T'ank ya fer this food, bless the hands that've prepared it, an' bless our stomachs which're ta receive it. We ask this in yer Son's Heavenly Name, Amen."

"Amen."

Paddy and his mother joined Paddy's father in eating the stew.

"This stew's good, Mother."

"T'ank ya, dear."

"Yes, it's very good, Finola, could ya pass me some bread?"

Finola Shannon handed her husband his second piece of bread and began to eat her stew.

"Now, Pádraig, I'm glad ta hear that y'ave been takin' care'f Bridget as I've asked, cuz that'll be yer job, summer long."

"Okay."

"I think now yer gettin' older, it's 'bout time start takin' some responsibility 'round the farm."

"Lochlan, he's only ten."

"I know how old my son is. He's old enough ta handle few chores."

"I will, sir."

"Good, good."

"I t'ink maybe he ought ta be runnin' 'round with th'other children. It's summer."

"He'll have plenty time run 'round once he's done his chores. 'Sides this'll keep y'out mischief, won't it, Pádraig?"

"Yessir."

"Good. Pass me some more bread."

With that, the elder Shannon ate the rest of the meal in silence, focusing on his stew, occasionally dipping bread with a firm stroke. Paddy and his mother kept quiet.

*　　*　　*

"So this is what the quizzical Danny Doyle does on a day off, is it?"

"It is."

Saraid found him sitting on the front stoop of his house, drinking a beer, reading a book. Danny smiled back at her. Absolutely breathtaking, you'd think that the sun rises and sets with her mood, that Sara.

"And you, Sara Doran, what keeps you busy on a day off?"

His smile grew.

"Oh, that's right; every day is a day off for you."

"Ooh, hit the nail on the head. Well done. I've just come by to see what you were up to."

"Reading."

"I can see that. What is it?"

"Kerouac."

"Any good?"

"You tell me, Sara, it's your book."

Daniél handed it to her. Inside the hardcover was a small inscription.

"I never did get around to reading it."

"I'll spare you the pleasure; it's damn good."

"Have any more of my books I haven't read you'd like to summarise for me?"

"A few, I'm sure."

"Like what?"

"*Heart of Darkness.*"

"How was it?"

"Best afternoon of my life."

"Anything else?"

"*Frankenstein.*"

"Scary?"

"Not as I imagined. Quite sad."

"But this Kerouac, damn good is he?"

"Yes, ma'am. I think you'd like it."

"And why is that?"

"Look at it."

Sara looked down at *On the Road* and it hit her.

"How long have you been reading it?"

"Well, I'd say I've probably read it about ten times over two years."

"That good is it?"

"Yeah."

"I like the colour you painted the house."

"Thanks."

*   *   *

Hello, Molly
It's good to see you again
I've been waiting
To say this for awhile

Oh, the times have been rough
And I've had it tough
But the thing that kept me going
Was you

*   *   *

"Oh, there y'are, Daibhead."

"Hey Da."

"Hello, Eoghan. Care fer some tea?"

"No t'anks, Tressa, I was jus' wonderin' if I could borrow Daibhead from ya."

"Sure, whaddya need?"

"I needya ta help me unload the van, I've only Marlene 'round and she's 'bout as helpful as - well, let's say she's not that helpful."

"Alright. T'anks fer tea, Nan."

"Yer very welcome, dear."

*   *   *

Fintan placed the knives on the red-hot element. The exhaust vent fan was sucking up most of the smoke, but he had unplugged the fire alarm, just in case. Niall Dugan was busy carving a plastic bottle to shape.

"They warm yet?"

"Almost, Niall."

"Alrigh', ya lemme know when yer ready."

Niall found Fintan to be an easy friend, always willing to go with the flow. Sorley had bailed on them that evening and was nowhere to be found. Fintan took a swig from his beer while he watched the knives heat up.

"Ready."

Fintan took the two knives and held them in front of Niall. His friend placed some hash on one of the knives and directed Fin to push the two knives together at their hotspots. As the smoke escaped from the act the makeshift bottle Niall held over the knives shepherded it all into his mouth. The two men took turns until the heat died down, and the smoke with it.

*   *   *

"So where'd ya take off ta last night?"

"Oh, out."

"Out, Daibh?"

"I walked 'long the river."

"That's a pretty long time ta be walkin' 'long the river."

"I guess."

Daibhead looked at his father bent over the pile of boxes and wondered how lonely he must be. Daibhead's mother had passed away ten years ago. Daibhead had been without Ánna for less than two weeks.

"D'ya miss her, Daibhead?"

"Everyone keeps askin' me that."

"Yeh, that's a question people ask when they don't know what else ta say."

"D'ya not know what else ta say 'round me, Da?"

"I don't know where ta start."

"D'ya miss Mum?"

Eoghan looked back at his son and smiled.

"I do. Immensely. No one's asked me that in awhile. T'anks."

"How'dya get over it?"

"I didn't. Yer mother is the love of my life. Ya don't get over somethin' like that."

"Well, does it get any easier?"

"You tell me, Daibhead. Do ya still miss yer Mum?"

"I do. I mean, I think I do. It's hard to tell."

"You were young. It's okay. Maybe it's gotten easier with time. But I know that one day I'll see her again."

"What was it about her that ya loved?"

"Everythin'. Grace was everythin' I could ever dream ta know
    'bout a woman. Women like her come 'round once in a
    lifetime. She was amazin'. She wasn't perfect, but damn
    she was perfect for me."

*   *   *

Sara sat on the couch and stared back at Danny as he filled her in
on all the town gossip from the past two years. She loved the
description and animation that he told stories with; he was
second only to Paddy in that regard. So much had happened in
the town since she had left and yet so little had changed. She felt
as if there was some strange sort of time warp where no one had
left, nothing had changed but they were all slightly older. Danny
had changed, though. Not a great deal, but there was a small
glimmer in his eye that Sara had noticed the first night she had
got back that was different. He seemed casual, as usual, but with
a sort of firmness around him. It was if he had become focused
over those two years, but on what still escaped her, and it
wouldn't surprise her if it escaped him, too.

Danny relayed the stories to Sara as if it had been the first chance
he had been given to let out all his knowledge. Working as a
bartender had given him a sidelined view on everyone's affairs
and he was known as a trustworthy confidante. He wasn't
known to gossip, but with Sara he held nothing back. Their
history had always allowed that. Danny had missed this part of
their relationship. Saraid Doran had been his best friend and that
was a gap that he couldn't fill.

"You're awful! I can't believe you're blathering on like a teenage
    girl!"

"Oh shut up, Sara, you love it."

She did. She loved every second of it. Danny was in as playful a
mood as she had seen him since she returned. He had been fairly
cool towards her the first couple days but had continued to open

up and today it was if it was the first time he had spoken to her without guard. It was one of those moments where all the history and hurtfulness didn't exist and they were just there, in the present.

5.
the colours of my affection

Nicolás awoke from his slumber and reached across the nightstand for his brushes. Right now was the time to paint and she had come to him in a vision. She – the most beautiful woman his eyes had never laid on (or so he thought). A canvas and her portrait were destined to meet. Of all the colours sprawled on his palette, only the deepest violet called out to him from the dream – the backdrop of his vision, a purplish cloud beneath the perfect form of her. Splash. On went the violet against the tan canvas, enveloping the surface as it had his mind. Without regard for the moistness of the under-layer Nic splattered on a pale cream for her skin, the violet seeping through as if her skin wore many bruises. A rich auburn brown was thrown atop her head, landing sporadically, creating a messy nest. Splat. On went a dark red, almost maroon, splotch, where her mouth ought to be. He was done. This eyeless woman, wearing bruises beneath her skin and indifference above herself stood on the canvas, naked, staring back at Nic. He knew this vision was his love. He must find her.

*　　*　　*

Danny Doyle hadn't felt this cheery in a long time. Today he was off to meet Sara Doran at the Shannon residence. It was a strange feeling to be so excited to see her as she was the woman who had once broken his heart, but over the last few weeks since she had returned to town they had rekindled their friendship and a missing part of him returned with her. Sharing gossip with her had been a wonderful, if slightly embarrassing, activity. Today was the first day he had spent any length of time in front of a mirror to get his hair just right. He blushed to himself that morning about it. He wore a collared shirt, as well, and had even ironed it, something he never did. It was in these little details that he worried the most, even though he knew that no one would notice any difference. No one, that is, but Saraid.

*　　*　　*

Fintan melted. His body felt like goo and he could barely move. He collapsed onto the couch and watched the television invade his mind. Niall was howling a terrible cackle. On the screen was a shark driving down the desert highway. This was all too intense. The stereo began to play and Fin needed to retreat beneath the couch to escape but found his corpse unable to cooperate with his brain. Circus bells and whistles created a disturbing cacophony between his ears and his eyes were being drawn into the dark images on the set. He was screaming to have Niall let him go. No words came out. Not one sound. All in his head. He just wanted to relax. What the hell? Niall Dugan's twisted face hovered over his own.

"I love this song!"

Too intense. Tense. Tense. His brain was shriveling up into the fetal position inside his skull and he was on his own. Somewhere in the midst of all this insanity he missed Sorley's fat, calming presence. Where was he? This was not the time to have abandoned his good friend, Fintan Larkin. How could he have left him here alone with this monster, Niall Dugan? Dugan was untrustworthy to say the least. They called him 'The Chemist'. What the hell kind of chemicals had he poisoned him with? Anthrax. He knew it. This was the kind of scary shit that kept security guards outside government offices at all times of the night. Where were they now? He needed them. He'd even pay his taxes if the bastards would show up right now and rescue him from Niall. Poisoned. Doomed. Fintan Larkin was going to die tonight inside Niall's flat on a stained brown couch. It would be an un-ceremonial ending, to say the least. How dare Dugan do this to him! Fintan had once been the best football player in the whole county. He wouldn't have done this to Roy Keane. Fuck Keane. Fuck Dugan. Fuck this. Fin contemplated his escape routes. The front door was six feet away. Too obvious. He looked to his right and saw the window that met the fire escape. Just give me twenty seconds to myself, Niall, and I am gone.

"What's your favourite song?"

Dugan was screaming something at him. Distract him, he thought. It's the only way he was going to be able to escape. Fintan opened his mouth and attempted talking.

"Drink, I need drink."

That will do, Niall will go to the kitchen and fetch him a can of ale from the fridge. Dugan obliged with Fin's concealed escape plan and left the room. Fintan tried standing up and his body betrayed him as he stumbled completely forward and landed face down on the floor.

"Larkin, y'alright?"

Niall's maniacal howling taunted him from above.

"Floor, I'm on floor."

Fintan's retreat from the death flat was foiled for the time being. As Niall helped him back onto the couch, Fin acquiesced and collapsed backwards. The movie continued to play on the television set and the horrific sounds from the record player continued to assault his ears. Feeling defeated, Fintan Larkin let the environment win and hazily melted into the sofa.

*   *   *

Pádraig woke with an ache in his back. This was becoming more common and the old man was feeling increasingly helpless. He had not wanted to trouble his son or grandson with the daily updates of his condition and had pledged quietly to keep it to himself. Eoghan had a hard enough time trying to run the pub without having to fret over his father. As for Daibhead, he could tell that his mind was a million miles away and any local requests would be filed in a cabinet in his skull to be discovered on some distant day. Because of these concerns for his boys, Paddy had continued to dress, feed and care for himself, much to his own discomfort, and occasionally, his dissatisfaction.

It was frustrating for Paddy, to think that not too long ago putting on a collared shirt would hardly be an exercise of his determination. Now, he had discovered, the almost infinite number of buttons posed a challenge to his failing dexterity. Behind the closed bedroom door each morning, Pádraig spent nearly ten minutes attempting to put on his beloved shirts. There were some days which were better than others, and Paddy was able to throw himself together almost effortlessly. More common though, were days where the patriarch would struggle to do up his shirt only to discover that he had misaligned the first set of button and hole and consequently wore a crooked shirt. Filled with a mix of anger and embarrassment, Paddy would have to undo all his buttons and begin again. Ties had long been abandoned.

Despite his back aching, today was altogether a good enough day and Paddy's hands slowly dressed him. After confirming with the mirror that his shirt was correct, and the rest of his wardrobe to match, Pádraig Shannon slowly swept a comb across his head, tidying his straight gray hair. Feeling confident with his appearance, he opened his door and exited his sanctuary to the rest of the home.

Heading down the hallway towards the kitchen, he noted the hanging clock, which displaying nine, let him know that Eoghan was already gone to tend to a variety of errands, Daibhead was most likely asleep still, and much to his anticipation, the family guest Sara was probably preparing breakfast in the kitchen.

Turning into the kitchen, he was pleasantly surprised to see Daniél Doyle sitting at the table, sipping coffee, while Sara was frying eggs and sausage. Pádraig noted a sweet smile on her face while she cooked and couldn't help but see Danny looking up from his coffee to admire her.

"Good mornin', Danny, a pleasure ta see ya here this mornin'. What brings ya by?"

Paddy chuckled to himself, knowing the attractively obvious answer was cooking breakfast.

"Hullo, Pádraig. I've just come to see lovely Miss Doran, here."

"And a good mornin' to you, Miss Doran, what is it yer makin' there?"

"Good morning, Paddy! I've got you some eggs and sausage. I hope you don't mind that I've scrambled your eggs."

"No, no, not at all. That's only my favourite."

"Well, I've even added a little spice to make a treat."

"Well, so long we don't tell Eoghan, should be fine!"

"Of course not, Paddy. That's why I'm here."

Paddy sat down next to Danny and Sara brought him a cup of tea.

"T'ank you, dear."

"You're very welcome."

It was at that moment that Daibhead dragged himself into the kitchen and plopped himself down at the round table across from Danny, with his back to Sara.

"Mornin'."

"Good mornin', Daibhead, sleep well?"

"Yessir."

"Good, good. Sara, have you enough eggs for the young'n?"

"Sure do, Paddy. How do you like yours, Daibh?"

"Scrambled's fine, Sara, t'anks."

"Daibhead, could I ask ya ta do me favour after breakfast?"

"Sure, Grampa."

"Could ya go o'er ta the grocery and buy me a copy'f today's
   Examiner?"

"I t'ought ya liked th'*Independent?*"

"I do. I like ta compare the two occasionally, though."

"Okay, I'll pick it up fer ya."

"T'anks, lad."

*   *   *

Staring down at the drafting table, Mícheál let out a secret smile
that no one would ever see. Before him were the blueprints for
his dream house he had just spent the whole night designing. He
had been reflecting on what his brother had asked him weeks
before. How could he be doing what he was doing without
worrying about it? He had no control over abandoning the
butcher shop, he still had to support his mother and going to
finish school was too much of a time commitment for him.
Glasgow was likely a distant possibility for him from now. He
could, however, still pursue his interests in his spare time. He
had always wanted to design towering residential buildings, and
it had been a long time since he had even thought about what
they would look like. But last night he thought about a far more
achievable project. He was going to design himself a new house.
He knew that he could design something spacious and yet
compact enough that his mother and he could both comfortably
live in it. If he was able to build it, they could afford to sell the
much larger family home they lived in now and still have some
money left over to help care for his aging mother. Who knows, it
might even be enough to give him the push towards finishing
school. The first step in all of this was the plans.

Possibility and reality were far closer in Mícheál Farrell's life
than he had imagined just weeks before. He had his dreamer
brother to thank for it all, but he wasn't going to share any of
this until he could calculate all the costs, dangers, and what-ifs.
Mícheál was far too rational to get carried away with any half-
brained dreams. Perhaps this time, he was getting excited with it

all, but he wouldn't dare break that news to anyone else, especially Nicolás or his mother, for the sake of propriety.

It would only disappoint his mother if he were to get her hopes up, both for the new home and his potential return to school, if he were to fail at both. The last thing he needed was his brother's encouragement pushing him and her; the sort of false hope that drove Nicolás was dangerous and with his mother's fragile condition potentially fatal. No, that would not do, Mícheál realised that the only way for this to go forward was in secret and only once all precautions were in place would he reveal his designs. That would surely be the best way to accomplish this, if it was indeed, accomplishable. What had been a smile on his face now turned to a frown as the enormity of it all weighed on him. No matter, he thought, it will take time and deliberation, precautions and preparation, thoughts and calculation, and perhaps he might make it all work. Yes, there was a faint light inside Mícheál that he accepted. But not now, Mícheál concluded, as he had to prepare for his day's work at the shop. Running on no sleep and burdened with the stress of his new ambitions, he changed into his work clothes and left.

*   *   *

Daibhead placed the newspaper on the counter and reached into his pocket for some coins to pay for it. After checking that his handful of change was correct he looked up and was surprised to see Natalya Abramov working where he had expected to see her father.

"Hullo, Natalya."

"Hi, Daibhead. How are you?"

"Good, how are you?"

Daibhead blushed. Natalya was a stunningly attractive girl, a year younger than him. She reminded him a lot of Saraid, in terms of appearance, though with darker hair. In personality she was far more reserved than Saraid could ever try to be.

"I'm well, thank you."

"I didn't know ya were working here today."

"Yes, Father has me working weekends. I've been doing that for the last month. When the school term is over, I'm going to be working much more, so he wanted to give me some more responsibility."

"Oh, that's nice."

"Maybe I'll see you come in here more often."

Looking at the attractive cashier, Daibhead was mentally trying to create a list of all the groceries he needed immediately.

"Maybe."

Daibhead paid for his grandfather's *Examiner* and left. At that moment he was wondering about how to thank Paddy for sending him over.

* * *

Sara led Danny down the riverside path. She very much liked his attempts at trying to dress-up without trying to show off. She noticed that the creases were ironed out of his shirt and giggled that his collar was not ironed at all and looked a little off.

"What are you giggling on about, Saraid?"

"You forgot to iron your collar."

"Damn, I knew I forgot something."

"It's okay; you look very dashing, despite it all."

"Dashing? Obviously, that was my intent all along."

"Well you succeeded, Mr. Doyle."

"Thanks."

"And…"

Danny looked at Sara and tried to guess what she wanted him to say.

"'And...' what?"

"*And* you look very attractive, Miss Doran."

"I don't think you are allowed to fish for compliments like that."

"I'm not? I thought the first thing that would have come out of your mouth would have been that. Here you go and disappoint me. Tsk, tsk."

He knew that she wasn't being serious. He had already thought about how gorgeous she was. Her golden hair shone in the sunlight and her skin had a faint tan that made her instantly more appealing than the pale skin that most women in town had. She wore a summer dress and a sweater that reminded him of when they first met.

She had danced then, as if floating above the ground, six inches above the meadows' dew, a magical whimsy in her smile, a disarming sword in her eye. She was the muse, the siren, the princess. When her dress twirled dervishly 'round, it entranced her admirers, locked on the sight that they saw; so close, so near, so very likely, something like beauty, that they had never seen before, nor were likely to be treated to again for the rest of their lives. And that's how she caught him there, in the meadow, and once he had set his eyes upon her, there would be no such freedom without her.

"You look very pretty, Saraid."

"Thank you! Now was that so hard?"

She laughed. Danny smiled. It wasn't hard at all. It had been something he had wanted to say to her since she had returned. Sara had also wanted to say something to Danny.

"I missed you."

Danny's face turned red and his smile grew, ever so slightly. Those words were the most precious things he had ever heard. It didn't take him more than a second to reply.

"I missed you, too."

Saraid looked back at Daniél and saw the face of the most honest man she had ever known. His words came out without effort and without any hint of bitterness. She knew she had hurt him and had doubted he would ever speak to her again, let alone say what she had wanted to hear. Somehow, through it all, Danny had kept himself together, and was here, with her.

"Can I ask you something, Danny?"
"Anything."

She hesitated slightly, and then grabbed his hand, and held it in both of hers. Looking straight into his deep blue eyes, she asked him the question she knew needed to be asked.

"Can you forgive me?"

Daniél had been waiting two years. During that time his emotions had seesawed. He had been angry, heartbroken and distraught. He had felt abandoned when he had needed her the most. She had been his best friend and had left him alone. Every inch of his body had poured out that first night into tears. Strangely, over those two years, he also felt better because of it. He had come to terms with Sara's decision to leave. It had matured him. He knew that through those great moments of despair he had become stronger. He had not let his emotions capsize him. He had grown up, and now, facing him was the cause of all that, asking for forgiveness.

"Yes. Yes I can."

"That means a lot to me, Danny."

Saraid's eyes were welling up. She had feared this day. She had never wanted to put him through the pain she had. It was the toughest decision she had made to leave him and leave town, that is, it was the toughest, until she decided to return. There had been so much water under that bridge since, and now, there was none, just a dried up riverbed, begging for renewal.

"I've enjoyed seeing you again."

"Me too."

"I didn't know what you were going to be like when I came back, but I am glad you've been as great as you are."

"Saraid, I can't help being like this. You were the brightest light in my life for a very long time. That never changed, even while you were gone, I missed you."

"I'm so sorry. I really am. I just had to leave."

"That's okay, I've already forgiven you."

Tears trickled down her face while she smiled back at him.

"Can I ask you a question, Saraid?"

"Anything."

"Why have you come back?"

She finally erupted with emotion. It was all too much, all at once.

"You! You! You! I need *you*, Daniél. I need you."

She put her face into his chest and cried. He wrapped his arms around her and closed his eyes, trying to remember every single detail of this moment. He kissed her hair and squeezed her tight, afraid that all of this was a dream. Her hands clasped onto the front of his shirt as her face was buried against his beating heart. Her hands, face and tears wrinkled his neatly ironed shirt, a concern that was far from the minds of them both.

6.
rejection hardly comes naturally

"Well then, tell us where y'ave been, Sorley?"

Sorley O'Mara grinned back at the eager faces of Fintan Larkin, Niall Dugan and Mícheál Farrell. He had been waiting for this opportunity what seemed like his whole life.

"Boys, I've got something to share with ya."

"Yes?"

"The other night at the club, when Fin and me went there, I met a broad."

"Well done, Sorley, we didn't think ya had it in ya."

"That I did, that I did."

"So… what's she like?"

"Oh man, she's wild. She's like the kinda woman ya find out in the jungle. Absolutely mental."

Mícheál was finding this hard to believe.

"Mental? Are you saying she's mad?"

"Fuck no, Farrell, she's jus' wild in bed is all."

"I wouldn't doubt if she had a mental illness she were sleeping with the likesa you, though."

The other two laughed at Mícheál's remarks. Fintan was especially disturbed at the thought that his friend had bagged the broad, when he, himself, had no luck that same night. His vicious laughter barely masked his insecurity.

"So does this wild jungle woman have a name?"

"Moira."

"Does she work?"

"Yeh, she's a teller at wunna the banks on the other side the river."

"How old is she?"

Fintan had remembered the woman hanging off of Sorley looking to be more than a few years older than him. He would have placed her in her late thirties or maybe her early forties.

"She's thirty-six."

The men howled at Sorley, not surprised that the only woman he could catch was most likely willing to settle for something less than perfect at this point in her life.

"Laugh all ya like fellas, but I'm th'only wunnus gettin' shagged."

"Maybe we could go round up summa her spinster friends."

"It's not that big a gap, I jus' turned thirty, last month."

"Yeh, but if ya took that gap in th'other direction ya could get a twenty-four year old."

"Fat chance that, Sorley couldn't get a twenty-four year old when he was twenty-four, what chance does he have now that he's old, fat and balding? Back then, he was only fat."

"Like you guys could do any better."

"Guaranteed."

Compared to Sorley, the other three provided quite a range of physical options for a woman. Fintan was certainly slimmer, verging on an almost anorexic thinness. This was only accentuated by his tall frame, which normally put him at least a head above most people. His horse-like face was a small improvement over the acned, waffle face of Sorley. Niall was much older than the others and his years of excessive drinking and drug use had caused him to age into an older, shorter, leathery version of Fintan. His eyes receded into his skull, sandwiched between his large nose and bushy eyebrows. Only Mícheál Farrell would be anywhere near the range generally known as attractive, that, even despite his slight beer gut, which drew attention away from an otherwise muscular body. His face was pleasant, if not dull, and well proportioned. He didn't typically hit on women so he was fairly unsure how he would perform under pressure, but he was confident enough that he had a far better chance than this lot.

"I'd like ta see you guys prove it."

"Okay, how?"

"Next Friday night, the group 'f'us go inta town, t'a club an' we'll have a contest."

"Whaddya mean the group 'f'us? Y'already got a broad."

"I'd come along as the judge."

"Y'aren't fit ta judge a competition."

"Whaddya mean I'm not fit ta judge a competition? Ya t'ink I can't figure out which wunna ya did best?"

"No, I just meant y'aren't fit. Ya might have a heart attack or somet'in' on the dance floor. It's liable ta cause us some problems. Ya would certainly ruin my chances 'f'I had ta 'company ya ta hospital."

"Sometimes I wonder why I'm yer friend, Fintan. Yer a real bastard."

"I t'ink ya jus' answered yerself, fatty. I may be a bastard but I'm th'only one that would hang aroun' with a fat slob like you."

Niall laughed away as Fintan hurled further insults at Sorley. Mícheál was beginning to realise why he rarely spent time with these idiots. He finished his pint and decided it was time to go.

"I'll see you lads later; I've got to check out."

"Where ya goin', Farrell?"

"Out."

With that, Mícheál left the blundering trio to continue their repetitive antics. He was going to go home and work on his project. It was late enough in the evening that his mother would have already retired to bed and he would be undisturbed in his study.

*   *   *

I've longed for this embrace
The look on your face
The moment we collapse
When all the walls are replaced
There's no time and no space
It's all history

It's so good to see you
Molly, I always knew
You'd remember me

And I'm not perfect
Nor are you
Or this old guitar
But it'll play a tune
A simple melody
Three chords repeat
Over and over again
And then...

*   *   *

Alan had been listening to Sorley's bravado. It was the typical kind of bullshit that he was used to hearing at the pub from the patrons. He often heard from them their sordid affairs and was generally disgusted with the way they acted. Certainly they must value women beyond the feudal tendencies they put on display with a pint in their hands.

Alan was in a mind to say something to Sorley about the way he had been speaking about his new girlfriend. Unfortunately, as he had been working up the courage to speak, the mob had shifted gears onto the topic of each of their conquistador abilities, each man had asserted himself and challenged Sorley's momentarily apparent superiority. Alan was going to interject, but, having seen Mícheál Farrell, his most likely ally, leave, Alan was faced with the prospect of insulting the rowdy group on his own.

"Now, ur, gentlemen -"

"What is it, Alan? Haven't we paid ya yet?"

"Um, no, that's not the issue."

"Well, fuck off then."

He was used to that kind of speak from Fintan and the gang and shrugged it off.

"I just wanted ta say, that is, I find it horrible the way ya speak 'bout women."

The accused just laughed. Niall looked directly at Alan and spoke.

"That's not a surprise, comin' from ya, Brennan; I doubt ya'd say anythin' mean t'yer gal pals."

"What's that supposed ta mean?"

"Y'aren't serious, are ya? I t'ought ya were queer."

"Me? Are ya daft? I'm not a homosexual. I love women. That's why I treat them with respect."

"And I'm sure that gets ya loads 'f'attention, yeh? Swimmin' in ladies, are ya?"

Alan didn't have a response. He hadn't been on a date, let alone done anything with a woman, in a long time.

"Well, Romeo, 't'ave ya t'say?"

"I still t'ink ya guys are goin' 'bout it all wrong. Women don't wanna be treated like groceries, ta be bought an' sold at will an' thrown out at th'end'f th'week."

"If she's all spoiled an' withered I ain't gonna eat it, son."

Fintan grinned and decided to join in the fun.

"I prefer eatin' out. Restaurants; the like. Why should I have ta buy groceries when I can go out an' be served somet'in' different each night?"

"Ya don't understand, ya stupid brutes! It's a metaphor. Women deserve far more respect from ya, but that's probably askin' too much at this point yer lives, isn't it?"

"Calm down, Casanova. Yer right up there in age with us an' haven't gotta lot ta show fer all yer respectful methods. I'm suspectin' that y'aven't even got with a woman."

"Have so."

"We've never seen it."

"Yeh, we've never seen y'even try. You should join us in our challenge next week."

Alan lost it.

"No! Absolutely not. That sorta behaviour is exactly what I'm talkin' 'bout. Ya treat women like pawns in some sorta chess match. Chess? No, not chess, yer too feckin' stupid t'attempt chess. Ya, ya treat them like it's a game of chequers."

Sorley laughed.

"King me!"

The others laughed with him while Alan's face was turning

rouge.

"Ri-ri-ridiculous! I can't believe ya guys."

"I can't believe y'aven't been with a woman."

"Have so! Ya just haven't seen it. I don't come in here, all fat an' stupid an' full'f myself talkin' 'bout it."

"Don't believe ya."

The three shook their heads at Alan in mock exaggeration. Huge grins beaming back at the frustrated bartender.

7.
an apple rarely falls far from the tree

Eoghan looked at his father across the kitchen table and saw a silhouette of the strong man who had raised him. His father was a frail old man, something entirely foreign to them both. When he had thought of his da, Eoghan Shannon always imagined a broad man with a fiery personality, nothing close to the elderly gent who now wore cardigan sweaters. Instead of tea, Paddy had always had a tumbler of whiskey in his hands. Instead of reading the *Independent*'s news section it had always been turned to the racing results. Old age and life had worn Pádraig into an altogether softer man than his son had ever known. Paddy had been the rowdy barkeep who shared licentious stories with equally shady townsmen and had laughed a hearty belly laugh at the most ridiculous tales. His one and only marriage had ended many years ago when his wife ran away leaving him with an infant Eoghan. Raising the lad on his own had been a chore best left undone. It was a wonder that Eoghan had grown into the capable man he was.

"How's yer tea, Da?"

"Fine, fine. T'ank ya, Eoghan."

"Anyt'in' interestin' goin' on'n th'world taday?"

Pádraig looked up from his paper and looked into the genuinely interested eyes of his son. Eoghan rarely cared about anything beyond his immediate vicinity and never picked up the paper, let alone ask about it from him.

"Yes, yes. Indeed, there are. Plenty'f t'ings. Plenty'f t'ings. Sad tales, many sad tales."

Paddy had been reading the paper for years, unbeknownst to his son, and had always preferred the world news section. The stories in far-off lands had always intrigued him. He had never traveled extensively and had always been curious of the larger world beyond Éire.

"What kinda sad tales?"

"Oh, plenty. Famine, disease, war. We're quite fortunate ta live where we do."

"That's so true. I've never thought about it that way."

"Big day taday, Eoghan?"

"No, nothin' special; jus' a few errands ta run. D'ya need anythin'?"

"No, no, no. I'm fine, t'anks. I t'ink I'll jus' spend my day listenin' ta radio."

"Ya could turn on the TV, Da."

"I prefer radio. It reminds me'f my father. We never had a television."

"Okay. Well 'f'ya need anyt'in' be sure t'ask."

Eoghan got up from the table, gave his father a short pat on the shoulder, placed his dishes to the side of the sink and left. Paddy sipped on his tea and continued to read the day's news.

*　　*　　*

Oh, sing for me
I've sung enough
For us both

Oh, sing for me
I've done enough
Sung enough
For us both

And when all is done
All the songs are sung
The end has begun
You'll sit back and see
There was you

There was me
And nothing beyond

Oh, I've done it all
For you
My love

Oh, I've done it all
For you
My love

And when all is done
When all songs have been sung
You'll see me
Smiling down on you
You'll see me
Smiling down, down, down

*   *   *

Sergei Abramov stormed into the bedroom with a fierce temper and began throwing books at the body lying prone in the bed.

"Get up! Get up!"

Maksim covered his face with his hands as books continued at him.

"Get up! Get up! Why don't you get up? You lazy boy! Get up!"

"S-s-sorry, Papa. I forgot to set the alarm."

"'Sorry'? 'Sorry'? You should be sorry! Now, get up!"

Maksim jumped out of the covers and stood in attention at his angry father, who had ran out of books to throw and now just stared at his son with an intensity that frightened Maks.

"You were supposed to be at the store an hour ago!"

"I'm sorry."

"Nobody was there to open the store!"

"I'm sorry."

"I got a phone call waking me up to open the store! 'Where was my son?' I asked."

"I'm sorry."

"'Sorry'? 'Sorry'? All I am hearing is 'sorry'. I've had enough. This is the third time, Maksim. I give you a job, I feed you, I put a roof over your head and all I ask is you work your shift. What do I get? I get 'sorry'."

"I'm so - I was up late studying for my exams. I went to sleep and I forgot to set my alarm."

"This, this, this is what they teach you at the university? I've been paying all this money to have you learn bad habits?"

"I'm so - it'll never happen again, I promise."

*   *   *

Paddy took out the small cardboard box from his closet and set it down on the nightstand. He opened it and looked at all the keepsakes he had held since he was a small boy. Through every trial in his life this small box had been his sanctuary. In his hands now was the only picture he had of Eoghan's mother holding the child in her arms before she left. Eoghan had never seen this picture, in fact, the only picture Eoghan had seen of his mother was in his parents' wedding photo, and he had only stumbled upon that by accident when he was helping Paddy move things into his home. Pádraig had decided that now was the time to give his son full disclosure on his mother. Eoghan deserved that much after taking him into his home. These sorts of things had never been easy for Paddy, but he knew it was the right thing to do, before time stepped in and made it an impossibility.

8.
a gentleman by any other name

"So, how was yer date?"

Marla's expectant eyes were burning a hole into Sara's face.

"It wasn't a date... well, perhaps it was; either way, it was nice."

"Yeh? Whaddya guys do?"

"We walked along the river."

"Ooh, well that does sound nice, don't it?"

Saraid smiled at Marla's apparent interest in her love life. It was nice to have a girlfriend to discuss these sorts of things with.

"I told Danny why I came back."

Marla's face went absolutely flushed.

"Ya did? Oh, no! What've ya done? Whaddya say?"

"I told him I came back because I need him."

"Ya didn't!"

"I did."

"And what he say?"

"He just held me. I think he whispered something similar but I couldn't hear him over my tears."

"Yer crying?"

"Well, yeah! It was a pretty emotional thing to say."

"Ya don't think would scare him off?"

"I don't think there's a thing I could do that would scare off Danny Doyle."

"Haha, probably marriage."

Saraid bit her tongue.

"Well, what's next for ya two?"

"I don't know. It's hard to tell. I'm not sure if he just wants to be friends. It's been so nice, just hanging out with him and aside from him holding me that one time there hasn't been anything romantic or anything."

"But that's what ya want, right?"

"Well I don't think I came all this way to make another friend."

"So whaddya ta do?"

"I think I might ask him if he wants to start up where we left off."

Marla just looked back.

"Maybe not. I don't know. I don't want to ruin anything. I really like Danny."

"Perhaps ya should just take it slow an' see where he's at. Y'ave only been back a couple weeks. Be a lot ta ask ta flip his world 'round like that."

"That's true."

As the two girls approached the pub's front door they looked at each other in a knowing way and completely shifted their conversation.

"Do you want to go shopping next weekend?"

"Sure. What are ya lookin' fer?"

"Probably some new shoes."

Inside the pub, Alan and Danny were working. It was a slow day and only a few patrons sat at a table in the corner. Sara sat down at a bar stool and Marla walked around the side of the bar and threw on an apron. Danny acted completely naturally and continued with his various chores behind the counter, pouring a fresh pitcher for the group in the corner. Alan looked up at the girls entering and went pink.

"Hullo, girls."

"Hi Alan."

"Nice day, isn't it?"

"It is. Shame you have to be inside working rather than outside enjoying it."

"Yes. Yes, it is a shame."

Marla smiled as she passed him on the way behind the bar. Sara continued the conversation.

"And what would you do on a nice day like this?"

"Oh, I dunno, prolly go fer a walk, or perhaps, if t'is really nice, take a trip ta the coast."

"That sounds nice."

Alan's pink face darkened to a shade of purple.

"Yes. Yes, that does."

Behind Sara, Alan could see Niall Dugan come wandering in through the door. He knew that this was his chance to show those idiots that he had what it takes to ask a pretty gal like Sara out.

"P-p-perhaps, 'f it isn't too awkward fer me t'ask, perhaps ya would like ta spend a day at the coast with me. I could bring a basket lunch with some wine an' we could make, that is, we could, go on a date, out 'f it."

None too smooth, but he knew that Dugan had overheard him. Danny had also overheard him, but his face only made a small smile that Marla could see. Sara looked at Alan with surprise.

"Oh, Alan, that is a lovely idea, but I've never really thought of you in *that* way."

Alan looked genuinely hurt. Dugan was now definitely within earshot and ordering a pint from Danny.

"What I mean to say, Alan, is that I've always thought of you as more of a friend and I don't think I could ever risk ruining that."

"Oh, okay. Well it's okay, forget me even askin', Sara. Wouldn't wanna jeopardise our friendship."

Dugan almost swallowed his ale down his windpipe. Alan glanced over at him and then turned back to Sara.

"Perhaps, if ya know any single gals, ya'd like ta set me on a date with 'em."

"Sure, Alan, I'd love to do that."

Alan Brennan left the bar counter and disappeared into the backroom. Niall Dugan erupted with laughter, which only lasted a short period when he realised he was alone. Marla hit him with a towel and told him to be quiet. He snarled at her and took his pint to a table beyond her reach where his smile returned.

*   *   *

Oh, Molly
Where are you now?
If I was to call you
Would you come?

Oh, Molly
Where are you now?
I've fallen on hard times

Would you come?

Oh, Molly
Where are you now?
I'm lying on the ground
Would you come?

Oh, Molly
Where are you now?
I'm crying in the dark
Would you come?

Oh, Molly
Where are you now?
I'm dying, dying
Would you come?

Would you come
If I called?
Would you come?

I need you to come

Oh, Molly
I need you
Oh, Molly
Would you come?

*   *   *

Niall waved Alan over to his table.

"Take a seat, Alan."

"I really shouldn't, Niall, I'm workin'."

"Look aroun', Alan, there're maybe ten people here an' there're three ya workin'. Take a seat."

Alan obliged.

"Alan, d'ya know what yer problem is?"

Alan began to think but was interrupted by the impatient Dugan.

"Alan, yer problem is that yer a fuckin' pussy."

"Excuse me!"

"Yer excused. Listen, no offence meant ta ya, but ya need ta learn how ta grow some balls an' be a bit more assertive. Otherwise ya might as well give up. Yer what, thirty-five? It's 'bout time."

"Niall, yer sayin' some 'credibly rude t'ings."

"Alan, I wouldn't do it 'f I thought ya had it in ya ta shut me up. But ya don't, do ya? Now, what I want ya ta do is go back ta Sara Doran an' tell her ya won't take no fer an answer, yer friendship be damned, yer gonna show'er a hell 'f'a time. Can ya do that?"

"I'm not goin' ta make a fool out 'f myself."

"Alan, 'f'ya don't go over there an' do this, yer a worthless piece'f carbon an' ought ta jus' drown yerself in th'river. What's the big deal? She's 'ready said no, she says no again what've ya lost?"

"'Side from any semblance'f dignity?"

"Alan! Jus' feckin' do it, already."

"No, tha's alright. I'm good. I've made a fool outta myself enough taday."

"I knew ya were queer, Alan."

Alan got up and walked away from the acidic Niall Dugan and returned to his work. He had heard enough out of him.

*　　*　　*

Fintan was pounding down drinks when Sorley interrupted him.

"Fin, it's time ta head in, mate."

"Feck off."

"Fin, I promised Moira I'd be back by midnight an' it's already half-two."

"Yer already whipped, ya sad fuck."

"That's enough! Alright, ya bastard? I'm headin' home."

"Fine! Good riddance. Still have Dugan."

"Dugan left an hour ago."

"He was right here. Jus' a minute ago. We were talkin' 'bout the Beatles."

"That was a long time ago. Dugan left an hour ago."

"I was jus' talkin' t'him! Are ya callin' me liar, Sorley O'Mara?"

Fintan stood up and threw his pint glass on the ground. The broken glass surrounded their feet. His bloodshot eyes scared Sorley.

"No, I'm not calling y'a liar. It's time ta calm down, mate, I'm goin' head home."

"Fine. Go home! Go back t'her. But don't ya dare call me yer mate 'gain! Ya heard me?"

"Fin, I don't know what's gotten inta ya but 'f'ya want me ta walk ya home on the way I will."

"I don't need ya! I can walk myself home!"

At this point Danny had come over to see what had happened as he had heard the shouting and broken glass.

"Fintan, Sorley, you guys alright?"

"I t'ink Fin's had enough, Doyle."

"Judas! Yer fucking Judas Is-*chariot*! Don't listen this venom-tongued arse, Doyle. I'll have 'nother pint, t'anks."

"Fin-"

"Shut it!"

Danny had heard enough. He called Eoghan over and the two of them, with Sorley's assistance, ushered Fintan Larkin out of the pub. Eoghan talked Fintan down.

"We're not kicking y'out Fin, we like ya, but it's time fer ya ta go home, 'kay?"

"Yeah, okay, Eoghan."

"Ya get some rest."

"Sure t'ing."

Fintan took off down the road, walking with a quick pace and a slight stagger.

"Y'alright, Sorley?"

"Yeah, Eoghan, I'll be fine."

"Take care an' get some rest."

"See ya, Eoghan. Bye, Danny."

Sorley slowly made his way down the road keeping his eyes on the breakneck Fintan ahead of him.

9.
a sweet cool breeze

"Oh, hullo, Daibhead."

"Hi."

"Can I help you find something?"

Daibhead looked at Natalya and shook his head.

"No, that's quite alright. I'm not actually here ta buy anything."

"Oh."

"I was wondering if ya wanted ta hang out sometime."

"I see."

"Don't get me wrong, I jus' mean as friends."

"Of course, you're still with Ánna, aren't you?"

"I am."

"Well then, sure, we can hang out. Come by later when I get off
and we'll hang out then."

"Great, I'd like that."

*   *   *

It seems you always find me
Like this
It seems I'm always in repair

I'm just another stranger
Like this
It's as if you were never here

Make my peace
Let this madness float away
Make my peace
I thought it would never get
Like this

I thought I'd always persevere

But I am just another weak man
Like this
I am on the outside left to stare

Make my peace
Let this madness float away
Make my peace

Take this madness and release

Make my peace
Let this madness float away
Make my peace
On a sweet cool breeze

*   *   *

"And, what is it you want now, Danny?"

"Sara, other than monogamy and trust, the only thing I want out of a relationship is handholding and the occasional neck massage. The rest is all a bonus."

"I'll hold you to that, Mr. Doyle."

"Deal."

Doyle meant every word. After all the tumult and shit that came with relationships, especially with Saraid Doran, there were very few things he could ask for. Monogamy and trust were the obvious requisites for a healthy partnership and the simple, almost childish requests for handholding and neck rubs were the manifestation of his simple and honest love. It was all he could give and ask for now. Beneath his light sweater beat a timid heart with a penchant for vulnerability. Danny had nothing left to hide from her, nothing left to protect, nothing that couldn't be crushed at her whim.

"Do you seriously want a relationship again, Danny?"

"No, not 'again'. I don't want what we had. I want a fresh start."

"I'd like that very much."

"And what is it you want, beyond that?"

"I'd love to take you away from here. Away, from all of *this*. I want you to see the world out there. I want you to come with me."

"Come with you, where? When?"

"Anywhere, anytime. Whenever you'd like."

"You just got here and you want to leave already?"

Danny looked at her with a look that floated between confusion and sadness.

"Don't look at me like that. I'm not leaving without you. Whenever you want to go. Not today, whenever."

"Thanks. I couldn't handle you leaving again. Not again."

"I know babe, I know."

Saraid took Daniél's hand in hers and stroked it softly.

"I just want you to see that there is more out there than just sitting around here, serving pints to this lot."

"They're good people, Sara."

"I know. But I want you to see museums, mountains, the works."

"Give me some time to think about it."

"Of course."

*   *   *

Nic sat in the corner of the pub and nursed his pint. The paper sat abandoned in front of him. He was itching for a cigarette but had quit smoking weeks ago. There was some sort of buzzing energy within him that he couldn't quite pinpoint, but knew was present.

He had been on a frenzied schedule lately, painting through the solitary hours of the night, inspired, possessed even, putting acrylic to canvas without regard for sleep nor food. His only concept of time was when the bar closed and he was told to head home, at which point his real day began. Nic, the night crawler; vigilante aesthetic.

"Another pint, Nicolás?"

"Sure, thank you."

Nic looked up at Marla's pale face, lit up by her bright red lipstick. It was *her*. Unbelievable, he thought, that she had been here all along, his whole life. The girl in the painting was Marlene Cullen.

"Ummm, Marla..."

"Yes, dear?"

"Uh, better make this my last pint."

"Alright then."

*　　*　　*

Natalya led Daibhead through the bramble patches to a clearing on a cliff overlooking the sea. She sat down near the edge and sighed.

"This is it."

"It's beautiful."

Daibhead looked out into what seemed like an endless abyss.

"D'ya come here often?"

"Usually once a week, or whenever I feel like getting away."

"I've lived here my whole life an' never known 'bout this place."

"Yes, because of the bramble most people don't venture up
    here."

"It's gorgeous."

Natalya looked at the boy and wanted to wrap her arms around
him but restrained herself, achingly.

"It is."

The sea mist began to dew their faces and they laughed childish
laughter and told each other tales.

10.
a harbinger of defeat

"It costs how much?"

Mícheál looked at the property agent waiting for a clarification from what he thought he misheard.

"Two hundred thousand euro."

He hadn't misheard. It was an outrageous and unexpected sum for him.

"But there's nothing here. It's a vacant lot."
"It is."
"I haven't even built the house yet."
"I know."
"And you are asking two hundred thousand?"
"It's actually a fairly decent price for the location."
"It hasn't even got a view of anything."
"No, that would be substantially more."

Mícheál's plans to build his dream home became far more distant than he had anticipated. How could this be? He had tried to anticipate every possible snag. This was far too much for him, even if he did sell his parents' house, it would barely cover the land and he'd have no money left to build. What good is a vacant lot?

*　　*　　*

Maks opened the grocery store door to find his father sweeping the floor. He took a deep breath and walked towards what he knew was a cyclone of emotion. The broom made quick violent passes over the linoleum surface. Sergei Abramov was in a trance, as if he were individually responsible for eradicating all semblance of dirt or grime in the world.

"I'm sorry I am late. The train was delayed coming back from the city."

Sergei did not look up at his son, continuing with his mission below his feet. Swish. Swish. Swish. Swish. Swoosh. Swish. Swish. Swish. Swish. Swoosh. The broom in his hands danced maniacally, small pieces of straw falling from the head.

"Papa, can I help?"

Maksim watched as the frenzied chore grew in intensity, fearing for the handle's life as his father was choking it. Sergei's hands were turning purple as they tightened around the long wood shaft, showing no mercy and little chance of acquiescence to the certain silent pleas it must have been weeping.

"Would you like me to take over?"

The sweeping just continued, sweat dripping from the older man's brow.

"Father, please, you've been working hard, let me..."

Maks reached in to take the broom from Sergei's hands but received only a protective elbow.

"Papa!"

Sergei stopped, turned to his son, his exhausted corps leaning on the broom, his face bright red and wet, and sighed.

"Get out."
"What?"

"Go."

"Go where?"

"Anywhere. Just not here. Not my store. Or my home. You are not welcome there either. Go anywhere else."

"What? Are you serious?"

"Yes, very serious. You don't want to be here. So don't be here."

"Papa, I don't know what to say."

"Say 'goodbye', that ought to do."

"'Goodbye'? What do you mean?"

"I don't want to see you around here. I want a son who honours his commitments. I want a son who understands the value of other people's time and effort. Go, please, just go. Come back when you are a man."

Maksim turned, opened the door and walked away, tears erupting down his cheeks.

*　　*　　*

Sorley O'Mara sat at the kitchen table, tea in hand, big stupid grin on his face when Moira joined him.

"Good mornin', Moira."

She just glared back at his fat waffled face, walked past him and poured herself a cup of tea.

"I like yer housecoat."

Moira Finnegan was not having any of this.

"Oh ya do, do ya?"

"Yes?"

"Well what is it, then? D'ya like it or not?"

"I like it."

"Good, good, ya fat fuck."

Sorley felt like a stampeding buffalo heading towards the cliff; he could see his impending doom, but was unable to turn around and avoid that tragic fate by any means. He grimaced.

"Somet'in' wrong, pet?"

"Ya have t'ask? What's wrong with ya?"

"N-n-nothin' that I know. Should there be?"

"Yer an absolute imbecile. Ya promise ta be home no later than midnight an' ya came crashin' an' bangin' 'bout the front door 'round three. Not only didya cause a commotion as ya rampage in ta the flat, but ya don't bother ta come in an' check on me."

"I t'ought sleepin' on the couch was a good idea, all t'ings consid-"

"Oh really! Ya t'ink, now do ya? What a startlin' discovery! Sorley O'Mara: capable'f independent t'oughts. Abso-fuckin'-lutely brilliant."

"Well, whaddya want me ta do?"

"I wanted ya home at midnight; that's why I asked ya be home at midnight. Is that too hard t'understand? Is yer thick skull not 'sorbin' anyt'in' I say? I'm not a bloody mystery. I told ya 'xactly what I want an' ya can't do that, or have decency ta call an' say ya'll be late."

"I'm sorry, I lost track 'f time. Fin an' Niall were eggin' me on."

"Oh, Fin an' Niall, then? Great. Gladya 'peased them. We wouldn't want Fintan Larkin or Niall Dugan t'ink any lessa ya, would we?"

"Wait, no-"

"Ya have t'always listen ta those two, do ya?"

"They're my friends, love."

"Don't 'love' me."

"Sorry, but they *are* my friends."

"Well, they're the wrong sort friends ta be hangin' 'bout. Hardly a good influence."

"Whaddya talkin' 'bout? Fin an' Niall are great lads."

"Oh really? We talkin' 'bout the same blokes?"

"What's yer problem with them?"

"What's my problem? My problem is that they're exactly the wrong sort people fer ya hangin' 'round with. I don't like the way they behave an' I don't wantya ta be actin' like that."

"What's wrong with the way they act?"

"D'ya really have to ask?"

"Yeah, I wanna know."

"Fine, let me spell it out fer ya. Fintan Larkin is an angry, racist, chauvinistic pig who drinks too much an' has no redeemin' qualities other than his apparent undyin' loyalty ta ya, which could probably be sold fer a pint an' a fag."

"Hey, that's not fair, that's not him t'all, ya don't know him like I do."

"Oh, sorry, should I know him like ya do? Should I have him borrow my money an' never pay me back? Should I have him drag me 'round the seediest places so he can risk my life? Should I let him batter me with insults an' cruel jokes? Tell me, Sorley, should I know him like that?"

"No, that's not true at all. We joke 'round together. I make as many jokes 'bout him bein' a twig an' a queer, s'all innocent."

"That don't make it right, Sorley. Ya shouldn't have ta put up his abuse an' ya shouldn't have ta justify actin' the same way. Yer better than that."

"No, Moira, I'm not. Fin an' I go way back an' he's like a brother ta me."

"And Niall Dugan, what is he? Yer long lost triplet?"

"Niall too? What is yer problem with him?"

"He's even worse than Fin! Dugan'll sell yer soul for a blippa cocaine. He's no real friends. He don't give a fuck 'bout ya, or Fin for that matter. He's a loser who only uses ya. Ya can't tell me he's a true friend. He's unreliable, untrustworthy an' an entirely selfish, acidic individual. Please, don't kid yerself 'round Niall Dugan."

"Well that's enough 'f'ya. I've heard enough shit 'bout my friends, t'anks. I'm goin' get some air. Ya need realise that I may've come home three hours late, but I came home ta you, Moira Finnegan."

*   *   *

The boulder dragged behind his body, slower as he walked up the slope of the walking bridge, until he reached the midpoint. Alan Brennan had decided that tonight was it. His clothes were soaked in sweat. The fifty-pound boulder had exerted a lot of energy from the normally lethargic bartender. His undefined and rather boyish physique hadn't anticipated the effort and was now aching.

"I can't believe people exercise, if they feel like this."

He spoke a low whisper to himself, talking himself through his tragic act.

"And so, after much disappointment an' failure 'n his mediocre life, Alan Brennan took his life inta his own hands an' drown himself."

He laughed a nervous chuckle to himself and thought that his eulogy was far too negative and in need of revision.

"Alan Brennan was a nice man. He was always very nice. Everyone always had nice things ta say 'bout how nice Alan was. N'one ever had anyt'in' not nice ta say ta Alan 'bout Alan cuz he was so nice. Alan was so nice that n'one knew a fuckin' thing 'bout him. Alan was so nice, he always took no ta mean no. Alan never grew a pair'f balls, oh, that's nice! Alan was nice an' will be missed by everyone for the duration 'f'his funeral, at which point they'll all return back their normal daily lives. How nice them ta take time outta their schedules, though, that was quite nice them. I'm sure we can all agree, Alan would've thought that the service was nice."

Tears were pouring down his cheeks as he lifted the boulder onto the railing and continued to revise his self-eulogy.

"Summaya may not know much 'bout Alan Brennan, so in order for ya fully 'preciate his tragic demise, let me tell y'a little 'bout him. Alan Brennan was born in Cork ta workin' class parents who took him ta church as a young lad. Alan loved goin' ta church an' enjoyed listenin' ta the stories 'bout Jesus an' his disciples. When he was ten he told a friend that he wanted ta be one 'f Jesus' disciples. That friend, someone Alan trusted more than anyone else told him that it was all a lie an' that the only thing the priests had in common with the biblical disciples was that they both enjoyed fishin' for men. Alan was devastated an' told his parents he didn't wanna go ta church ever again for fear the priests. It wasn't much longer than that when young Alan was watchin' the television an' a news story came on reportin' 'bout a priest in America who'd been found guilty touchin' altar boys. This, course, only fueled young Alan's imagination an' every priest he saw was jus' a pedophile in disguise. He never entered a church again."

Alan sat on the edge of the bridge facing the water with the boulder beside him.

"There are a few regrets that Alan Brennan left behind on earth. He never found love. That is a big one. He never found happiness. He never found peace. He never found anything close. He always suspected that 'f'he could find wunna those three, the others would follow. Sadly, none'f these regrets were ever resolved."

Alan smiled and said what he thought was his final eulogy.

"Alan has always been a searcher. He has searched for love in all corners this world. He has tried ta bring happiness t'others, so that happiness would be bestowed on him. He has wrestled demons an' now he'll find his peace."

Alan pushed the boulder off the edge of the bridge and watched it fall, waiting for the rope to fully extend and pull him with it.

*   *   *

If there is no more you
Then there can be no more me
By God you know
I'm going to float down the Liffey

11.
we laughed, we cried, we lived, we died

Daibhead sorted through the mail with a casual air about himself until he came to an envelope addressed to him. His girlfriend's name in the top left corner turned his relaxed nature into something verging on glee. (You know that feeling? Of course you do). Rather than race to open it he held it in his hands and contemplated when and where the appropriate moment should occur. He had promised to help his father in the pub in five minutes and didn't want to be late, however he also knew that his work rate would be lacking if he were distracted wondering about his letter. Daibhead Shannon decided that it was best that he open it up and read quickly and then return to look at it in further detail later, after his commitments were fulfilled.

"Dear Daibhead,

I hope all is well with you. I have been having an amazing time so far. Africa is fantastic. I absolutely love it here. I don't know how I lived life before I came here. It's truly amazing. I don't think I'll ever want to leave!

My family I am staying with are super nice and have been extremely hospitable to the white girl from Ireland. They call me the white daughter. It's really funny. They have four kids, ages five to eleven, and we all get along so well. The little one calls me 'Nana Ánna', it's really cute! I've been helping the father around the farm and can now say I am no longer just a useless town girl. I even wear rubber boots, which is a crazy fashion faux pas, but doesn't matter at all here! I love it. I've been taken care of so well. The mom makes these awesome African potato dishes all the time and suffice to say I haven't been starving! In fact, I think I have even put on a little weight, but that's cool because you know how black people like a little meat on their bones..."

The letter went on but Daibhead put it down and went down to the pub to work. He was glad to hear that Ánna was alright.

"Oh, hi Da, how are ya?"

"I'm well Eoghan, t'anks."

Pádraig Shannon sat down at the table. His sweater, despite the warm weather outside, betrayed the chills his frail body felt.

"I'd like ta have a word with ya, son."

"Sure, go 'head."

Paddy reached under his sweater into his shirt pocket and pulled out the worn photograph.

"This is yer mother, Maeve, my wife."

Eoghan took the photo in his hand and stared coldly at the unfamiliar face holding the infant in her arms. That infant, him, had no idea what would happen next in his life. He had no idea who his mother was. He had no clue why she would leave or where she would go.

"She was so young."

"Yes, I was quite a bit older than her. About fifteen years older, I reckon."

"Tell me 'bout her."

"Are ya sure?"

"Of course! I've wanted ta know so much about her my whole life."

"Maeve Hogan was a girl I met when I was in Dublin. I had been workin' at the shipyards an' ran inta her when she was waitressin' at a pub in Temple Bar. She was a pretty little t'ing. It was love at first sight. I had never believed in that sorta t'ing an' bein' in my thirties I didn't s'pect much ta change in that respect. Well, I met Maeve an' all that changed. She was confident in herself, she loved ta chat with me about anyt'in' an' everyt'in'. I was real enamoured with her an' we started goin' together. Now, in those days, it wasn't the type 'f relationship that they'd call decent, no, there were many nights where we were sneakin' inta each other's buildin's ta see each other. She had a real severe roommate, a woman 'bout forty, who had left a convent only recently. Well, she wasn't a nun nomore, but she was still a pious woman an' didn't like what she 'spected was goin' on in the wee hours the night. One mornin' she came inta Maeve's room, unannounced an' found us there. She threw Maeve out the flat, on the spot. Couldn't make much fuss 'f'it, could Maeve, cuz how Catholic t'ings were back then, far more strict than now."

"Wow, Da, I had no idea."

"I know, a real rebel, yer old man. Stickin' it ta the Church by stickin' it ta- never mind. Lemme get back ta the story. Well, I took Maeve t'a friend's house an' she stayed there with his wife an' him while we planned our weddin'. I didn't mind rufflin' a few feathers but I knew enough 'bout Ireland ta know that a man in his thirties an' a young girl weren't ta be messin' 'bout without 'tendin' ta marry. After six months courtin', Maeve an' I married. She was eighteen at the time, I was thirty-three."

"I had no idea she was so young."

"Yes, very young. Her father was only a few years older than I was, maybe forty at the oldest. When I met Eoin, that's yer namesake, her father, he was more than a little taken aback."

"I was named after my grandfather?"

"Ya were."

"An' ya couldn't tell me this before? Dad, I'm forty-three, I've had my whole life covered in cloudiness an' unknowns an' ya couldn't tell me these small, but meanin'ful details?"

"I'm sorry, Eoghan, I really am. Lemme finish the story an' hopefully you'll understand why I didn't tell you any'f this before."

"Fine, please go on."

"The first year'f marriage was absolute bliss. I had been given a decent raise on the shipyards an' yer mother could 'ford ta stay home an' take care the flat. It wasn't anyt'in' fancy but it was ours. T'was jus' after our first anniversary when we found out that we were goin' ta have ya. Honestly, the happiest moment in both our lives. I held a massive celebration at our flat an' invited yer mom an' I's friends from all over. I even had cousins from the countryside come inta the city. After that, I worked as much overtime as possible ta save as much money ta get ya started out in life right. We bought a crib for ya, brand-new, from a store. I was so proud. Me, the shipworker, the newly married man, buying a brand-new crib. The people in the store were so amused with how excited I was."

"Was a new crib really that bigga deal?"

"Oh, course. I was the first person I knew that bought one brand-new. All our friends had one passed down from their parents or siblin's. We were the first ta get a new one. Real status symbol, that crib."

Pádraig paused for a moment, took a sip of water, and continued.

"When ya were born, I knew that I had fulfilled my role in life. There was not'in' more important fer me than ta be a father. As ya can imagine, being so much older than yer mother, there had been a declining window 'f opportunity fer me. Ya came an' I knew that I was a man."

"An' my mother?"

"She didn't have the same experience, I'm afraid. There's a lotta details that are still foggy 'round that time, but please rest 'sured that ya were not the sole reason she left. But she did leave three months after ya were born. Maeve was not the same when she came home from the hospital with ya. She wasn't the same vivacious an' fun woman. She wasn't confident. She rarely wanted ta speak with me nomore 'bout anyt'in'. She just sat in the bedroom, the lights off, an' slept most the day. I didn't know whether this was normal or not. I had never been 'round new mothers. I tended ta ya as much I could. She put ya on bottle almost immediately. I didn't know any different. She became angry an' yelled at me. I stole her youth, she said. I was the man responsible for suckin' her youth from her. She wanted it all back. She wanted her youth back. One night I came inta yer nursery an' she had put a pillow over yer face. I snapped. I pushed her away from the crib an' lifted y'inta my arms. You were crying, but still breathin'. I yelled at her. I asked why she would do such a t'ing ta ya. She sobbed away that she wanted ta forget that any this had ever happened. We sat together on the floor, you in my arms an' I talked her back ta reality. She said she was sorry. All this was too much fer her. She was only twenty."

"Oh my God. She tried ta kill me."

"I told her ta go sleep. She went t'our bedroom an' closed the door. I sat with ya through the night. I wouldn't let go ya an' I wouldn't close my eyes. I didn't know what else ta do. When the mornin' came I opened my bedroom door ta find an open window an' a pile'f clothes thrown on the floor. Most the dresser drawers were still full, but t'was 'parent 'nuff that Maeve wasn't comin' back."

"An' that was it?"

"That was it."

"Did y'ever hear from her again?"

"'Bout five years later. I got a letter from her. She was livin' with her aunt in Donegal. She had met a man an' was askin' that I sign the divorce papers so the two them could make it legitimate. I signed an' mailed them back ta the post office box address she had given me."

"I'm sorry ta hear that. Did ya hope that she would have come back?"

"No, actually. I hoped she would never come back. I didn't want ta hear 'nother t'ing from her so long we both lived. I guess I got my wish."

Pádraig took a newspaper clipping out of his shirt pocket and handed it to Eoghan.

"Is that her?"

"T'is."

"'On January 17th, 1970, on the road between Donegal and Sligo, near the town of Tullaghan, a passenger car lost control in the rain and collided with an oncoming transport vehicle. The driver of the lorry was rushed to hospital in nearby Bundoran, and is in stable condition, however the passengers of the car, Maeve Hogan, 24, and Gaibrial Donegan, 25, both of Donegal town, did not survive the impact of the collision. Hogan and Donegan were engaged to be married June 18th. Further details on a memorial service are forthcoming.'"

"They had the funeral three days later. Her aunt invited me. I declined."

"So that's it."

"That's yer mother's story."

"T'anks. I needed ta hear this."

*   *   *

Sleep, I can sleep, now
At last
And rest, just rest, now
At last

All the things I ever wanted
Everything I ever desired
Gone, gone, gone

So sleep
Sleep, you know, you should
Sleep, just sleep
And let it rest

All the things I wanted
Everything I ever desired
Out of reach, forever
Tell me what's left?

Sleep, just sleep
All those dreams
Sleep, just sleep
And let it rest

There is nothing left
So let it rest

*   *   *

The laughter dug into him. How could they be laughing? There was nothing funny about this at all. He had bore his soul to them and they just laughed.

"Ya mean, ya dragged a boulder ta the top 'f the footbridge an' threw it off with a rope attached, with the 'tention 'f drownin' yerself?"

"Yes! This is what I am tellin' you all."

"But ya forgot ta tie the boulder ta yerself."

"I did."

They erupted with laughter. Alan's failed suicide attempt was not taken seriously by anyone. It merely provided fodder for Niall Dugan and Fintan Larkin.

"Wow, if ya wanted ta kill yerself before, ya sure must feel like a failure now."

"Yeah, Alan, yer not very good at anyt'in'. I can't believe ya forgot ta tie the rope ta yerself."

"T'anks. That's very kind of ya."

"What kind of eejit would tie a boulder with a rope an' drop it off a bridge an' not tie t'himself first?"

"T'anks."

Alan's face was burning red and his looks of desperation were only being met with more sarcasm and laughter. The cruel marauders of character drank ale and crushed spirits at will.

"Oh, don't cry, ya queer, nobody wants ta see that."

"Yeah, how 'boutya grow a pair an' move on with life. Ya didn't kill yerself so now ya can get me another pint. Cheers, mate."

Alan threw the empty pint glass at the wall.

"Ya think I'm kiddin'? Ya think I want ta be here? I wanted ta kill myself. I have nothing ta live for an' none 'f you are giving me any reason ta believe otherwise."

"Whoa, settle down there."

"No, don't tell me ta settle down. Yer a bunch 'f assholes. All 'f ya."

Sorley O'Mara looked around at the laughing faces on Niall and Fintan and realised he wasn't laughing with them.

"Didya really want ta kill yerself, Alan?"

"Yes, Sorley, I did."

Alan let tears fall down his face. Niall snickered. Fintan tried hopelessly to hold back a smile. Sorley looked at his two friends and then at the bartender. He couldn't help but feel sorry for him. He couldn't believe that the other two were acting this way. Did they have any feelings themselves?

"I have ta go."

Sorley got up and walked out of the pub.

"Fat queer."

"Probably goin' home an' cry in his pillow."

"Yeah, don't worry, Alan, you'll still have Sorley ta be gay with."

The two laughed and ordered another round of drinks. Alan threw his towel on the counter and went to the backroom.

12.
whom to blame but ourselves?

"I'm sorry."

Moira looked up to see the lumbering figure of Sorley O'Mara leaning over her.

"Y'are now, are ya?"

"Yes. Yer right."

"Was I? Right 'bout what?"

"Fin an' Niall. Yer right. They're arses."

A small smile came over Moira's face. She took Sorley by the hand and sat him down next to her.

"That don't mean they can't be yer friends, love. It jus' means ya
 need ta keep yer head on straight 'round them two."

"T'anks."

"I know they mean a lot ta ya."

"They're my friends. They're jackasses, but they're my friends,
 too. I jus' don't want ta be like that."

"Yer a good man. I know y'are."

"Are we okay now?"

"Yes. 'f course. Try ta keep yer word an' be home when I ask an'
 we'll always be okay."

"I wanna be that guy."

"Don't be that 'guy'. Be that *man*."

"Okay."

"I love ya, Sorley."

"Really?"

"Yes, really. I'm truly, madly, deeply in love with ya."

"That's all I've ever wanted."

"I'm right here."

*   *   *

You can't help me
I'm drowning
I'm sinking
Beneath

You can't help me
I'm drowning
I'm choking
Can't breathe

You've drowned me

Take back your thoughts
Take back your feelings, too
Take back your words
Take back everything from you
Because I can't breathe
You've drowned me

Molly, I'm sorry
But you're no good for me
Molly, I'm sorry
But I gotta ask you to let me be

I can't take a single moment more
Take back your memories
I'm sinking
Somewhere beneath

*   *   *

"What's eating your brain, Daibh?"

"Oh, hi Danny. Jus' t'inkin' 'bout t'ings."

"Yeah, I can see that. You look as if yer head were about to explode."

"It might. I'd prolly welcome that at this point."

"Things with Ánna?"

"Yeah."

"It's tough."

The two young men sat there staring out the window.

*   *   *

"Yer a despicable weasel."

"Hullo, Alan. Nice ta see ya too."

"Fuck off, Dugan."

"Can I interest ya in a conversation, Alan?"

"I was on that bridge. I had the boulder in my arms an' I let it drop cuz I knew that it would take that smug look off yer stupid face. An' one fuck-up later an' I am here an' yer smile is jus' gettin' wider an' wider. What is it with ya that makes ya so fuckin' smug?"

"Guess I was born this way."

"Is that so? Jus' like I was born queer, is it? Or somethin' else y'always like ta rag on about?"

"I dunno if ya were born queer or not, but somethin' 'long the way sure has made ya that way. Maybe we could head o'er ta the university. Take some tests. Settle the old nature versus nurture debate right now."

"I hate you! Yer an absolute asshole!"

"No need ta spaz out there, Alan. Use yer inside voice."

Alan grabbed Niall by the throat.

"Now ya listen ta me. I'm not takin' nomore 'f'ya or anyone else's shit from here on out. D'ya understand?"

101

Niall looked petrified.

"Do ya understand?"

"Y-y-yes."

*   *   *

"What's going on with her?"

"I dunno. I got a letter th' other day."

"You haven't had a chance to talk over the phone?"

"No, she's in a real remote area an' it's expensive as hell ta call an' the signal's unreliable."

"What the letter say?"

"She's havin' the best time'f her life."

"And that bothers you?"

"It does."

"Why's that?"

"Cuz what does that say 'bout all that time with me? Was it all shit?"

"I don't think it was."

"Then why would she say t'ings like that."

"I don't think she meant it that way."

"Well, feck, what am I ta t'ink? I'm letting my insides get all turned about. I can't stand this."

"Do you love her?"

"Yes."

"Does she love you?"

"Yes, I think so."

"Then just wait it out."

"All summer?"

"All summer."

"I don't know, Danny, it's a long time."

"It is."

"It's so hard."

"It is."

"And ya t'ink it's worth it?"

"Everything is worth it."

"What's that s'posed ta mean?"

"Daibhead, if you really love her, you need to let her find herself. She's gone to the most remote parts of the world because she needs to get lost. She needs that. What do you need?"

"I need her."

"Well, if you think that's it then go to Africa. She's there."

"No, I don't t'ink that's the t'ing ta do."

"And why not?"

"This is her time ta figure t'ings out fer herself."

"Exactly. Which means you need to take this time to do the same."

"Feck, I wish it were easier."

"Nothing is quick or easy."

"How didya manage ta survive bein' 'way from Saraid fer so long?"

"I didn't."

"But ya guys are back together now."

"Yes, but when she left two years ago she left a very different person. He didn't survive. I'm somebody else now. If she loves me for this..."

"Yes?"

"If she loves me for this then maybe a small part of that old me might come back to life. But I'm not sure I want or need that right now."

"Whaddya want?"

"Same thing I've always wanted: love."

"An' ya t'ink you've got that this time?"

"I can only hope. Without hope, nothing."

"Are y'afraid gettin' hurt again?"

"I've got nothing left to fear."

"Really?"

"Really. But enough about me. This was supposed to be about you."

"Well you've calmed me down a bit. I don't know 'f I can do this but I t'ink I know who ta come ask fer advice when the ocean gets rough."

"Go ahead, but you'll get more outta million other people. I'm just me."

"Yer good at it."

"Thanks."

"So I'm jus' goin' ta wait this out."

"Figure things out."

"The summer without Ánna."

"The summer without."

13.
i'll have a pint of the dark stuff

I spent a long time, myself, thinking about what to do, on my own. You'd be surprised how refreshing it is to lose yourself. No fear, no worries. Just a man, wandering, wondering. Molly, things could have been so different. I suppose, even now, we can sit and drink and contemplate the present. You've lost your boy, and I, myself. I don't think either of us could have predicted this many years ago, and yet, here you sit, and drink patiently while I unravel more and more of this yarn, trying to tell you what I found when I lost myself.

I guess, the biggest change for me to get there was to let go of my apprehensions and my hang-ups, to become free, to become lost. I know I don't look like much anymore, wearing these rags, with my beard grown out, and whiskey on my breath, but you shouldn't judge me. You know me. Or, should I say you knew me. I'm no longer the busybody, the nine to fiver. I've become a bit of a wanderer. I think you've caught on, Molly, but your face isn't showing it. You want to know. It'll come as the story unfolds, I hope, if I tell it well enough, and my memory doesn't fail me.

For most of this story I sat with my back against the wall and with my ears to the ground, do you understand? *I was there.* As things go on, we search for historians, storytellers, cataloguers, and what-have-you. Lo, who are you to trust, in these days, with the tale, the account of goings-on? Do you look to the busybodies who go from A to B, or the outdated flaneur that strolls the boulevard searching for some lost aesthetic? Heed the words of those dandy fellows, for their minds are focused on the oft-ignored and forgotten. Think: when the average man rushes to work, who is left to smell the roses?

Do you get it, Molly? In order to find myself, I had to lose myself. In order to understand what's going on, I had to withdraw from society. I had to melt into the brick walls like some sort of mortared wallflower. Oh, but how could I withdraw from society? I couldn't, *I was there.* Even if society would wish to exclude me, the ragged singer, it cannot, nor can I. I am a part of a living organism. The troubadour sings of the times. His voice is the beating pulse of the nation around him. And what is our zeitgeist? Listen to the whispering lyrics. It is a crying out for help. Somewhere, anywhere. We all just want something. We are a hungry folk. Begging to be fed with something like bread.

*   *   *

Sergei Abramov sat in the armchair while his wife paced back and forth in front of him, occasionally exclaiming random outbursts.

"Well! I can't believe it!"

"Natasha, control yourself!"

"How can you ask me to control myself? My Maksim is out there! You've thrown him out to the wolves."

"Wolves? What wolves? He's not living in the forest. He's staying with a friend in a Dublin flat."

"A Dublin flat! Even worse! Oh, Sergei, the city influences! The bohemians!"

"Natasha, please!"

"The drugs! He's going to be a drug addict, begging for change on Grafton to get his fix!"

"Maks doesn't do drugs."

"No, not the Maks we knew. But the new Maksim, the one who was thrown onto the street by his heartless father. He does drugs!"

"Relax, this is a good experience for Maksim. He needs to become a man."

"A man? What kind of man do you want him to be? A cruel man like you? Sending your firstborn out into the cold, without so much as a sweater to keep himself warm while he's huddled in a shop doorway at night, sleeping on the street? Is that what you want?"

"You are overreacting."

"Overreacting? I am most certainly not overreacting! If anything you are *underreacting*. But I shouldn't expect much from that cold heart of yours."

"He'll be fine."

"He'll be stabbed."

"Now that is just absurd."

"Stabbed in Phoenix Park. He'll be walking through there in the middle of the night and he'll be stabbed by some lunatic. You know the type that wanders around there in the dark. Stabbed in Phoenix Park! Oh my boy! Lord protect him!"

"Do you know what you sound like?"

"A concerned parent. Something you know nothing about."

"He's twenty years old. He'll survive."

"Survive? *Survive*? Like a bomb exploded in a shopping mall and three people survived? I can't imagine my Maksim-"

"You never had any issues with him traveling to Dublin before for classes."

"Oh, but that's the daytime. Everyone is so reasonable in the daytime. Not at night. Not in Phoenix Park."

"What is Maksim going to be doing in Phoenix Park in the middle of the night, Natasha?"

"Looking for his heroin."

"He's not a drug addict."

"Not yet! Not yet, Sergei! But you've sent him to the wolves!"

"He had to move out at some point."

"Oh I know, but with a little bit of warning. I could have warned him about Phoenix Park."

"He knows about Phoenix Park."

"Oh, of course he does, he knows that's where he can get his fix.

I can't believe I raised a heroin addict. Well, we're never letting Natalya out of our sight."

"That's crazy. You are being crazy. Maksim is not a drug addict and we are not going to treat our daughter like a prisoner because you think our son is in Phoenix Park buying heroin."

"Forgive me. I've been such a horrible mother. I wish I could have seen the signs."

"Signs? What signs? Maksim has been selfish and missed work numerous times and I decided to teach him a lesson about responsibility. He's not a drug addict and he's not in Phoenix Park in the middle of the night."

"No, no, of course not, he's in Temple Bar, busking for spare change. He'll buy the heroin in the daytime with whatever money he can earn busking outside the pubs. Oh, I wish I had taught him more songs on the guitar. He's going to have a very hard time with what little he knows. Of course his bohemian friends will teach him folk music. Does folk music make good coin, Sergei?"

"Natasha, Maksim is not going to be busking in Temple Bar, begging on Grafton Street, or stabbed in Phoenix Park. He just needs to learn some responsibility. He's going to have to find a place to live, get a normal job to pay rent and become an adult. He'll be fine. This is good for him."

"Well I can tell you I won't be going to his funeral when he is stabbed in Phoenix Park."

*   *   *

Be my downfall
Be my shame
Oh please, won't you
Be my Kitty O'Shea

I'd throw away my ambition
Throw it away
I'd throw away my success
And all my fame
I'd throw away my pride
Pride and my shame

Be my downfall
Be my shame
Oh please, won't you
Be my Kitty O'Shea

I'd throw away my power
Throw it away
I'd throw away my position
And my own name
I'd throw away all my hopes
I'll let them fade

Be my downfall
Be my shame
Oh please, won't you
Be my Kitty O'Shea

I'd throw away my ambition
And the hopes of a nation
If you'll only be
My Kitty O'Shea

*   *   *

The letter stood out from the other mail on the table. Taunting and calling her to open it. Tressa Bradigan could not take anymore. She tore open the envelope and read what she already knew was handwritten heartache.

"Tressa, ol' girl, times have been tough, I know, but I hope this finds you healthy and spry as ever. I've been traveling a lot and have finally found a place to settle here on Koh Phenang. It's absolutely gorgeous and I think I may stay forever. I've met a girl here, a local, and she

wants to marry me. I told her that's a bad idea, well, you know me, anyways the young thing talked me into it and we're having a quiet ceremony on the beach next month. All her family is coming. Well I thought I would mention it to you and you can pass it on to the rest of the family that I am well and that you are all with me in spirit.

I think it's best that we cut all ties as I begin my new life here. It's time I move into a different phase in my journey and I hope that you are able to do the same. Please forgive me for not including a return address, but it is best this way. Also, you'd probably feel obliged to send something for the registry and we haven't even picked out a hut to live in, yet worry about the decor. Just a little humour. May many blessings flow your way.

Much peace and contentment,
Liam"

So many tears covered the thin onionskin paper the letter was written on that it became opaque. The moisture turned it into mush in her hands and was thrown to the ground so that she might hold her weeping face.

*   *   *

"It's a bad day, taday is."

Eoghan held his father's wrinkled and spotted hand. He was choking back emotion as he looked at the pale impersonation of the man who had raised him.

"They keep gettin' harder."
"Don't. Don't talk like that. Please, Da, don't."
"Eoghan, son, the Lord will take me when He is ready."
"But not taday. Not taday. He's not ready. I'm not ready."

Pádraig smiled at his son's impassioned words.

"That's not for us ta decide."

"Da-"

"Cheer up, Eoghan, taday is jus' a rough day, but I t'ink we'll get through it."

"We will."

"Yes, course. An'f we don't, t'is time. I'm not in charge the meter an' there're only so many coins ya put in 'fore ya run out."

"I'll find some change, Da. I'll spot ya some change."

"I wish t'were that easy. We can't trade in our old jars'f pennies now."

"Have ya been feelin' like this a lot, lately?"

"I have. More an' more frequent. I haven't been gettin' up as much."

"Has Daibhead noticed?"

"No, not likely. He's been a busy boy, rushin' 'round. Tryin' ta keep his head an' his heart intact."

"Let's not upset him 'til it's time, 'kay? Promise me that?"

"I'll promise ya nothin'. I'll not hold back anyt'ing from my grandson."

"We've still got some time, let's not worry him anymore than we ought."

"Yer doing plenty'f worryin' fer us all."

14.
a rest is as good as a change

"So-"

"'So-' what?"

"When are we running away to La Rochelle?"

"Settle yourself down, Saraid. I need sometime to get things in order here before yer dragging me to the Mediterranean."

"La Rochelle is actually on the North Atlantic."

"You see? I need to do some studying first."

"Danny, are you afraid of me?"

"There's nothing left to be afraid of."

"What's that supposed to mean?"

Daniél's eyes flashed in front of Sara's. This was not a man whose fear was to be questioned in a trivial manner.

"When you loved somebody so much, for so long, and they mean absolutely everything to you, when that person has your heart in their hands and they walk out on you, there is nothing left to fear."

"Daniél-"

Saraid put her hands on his cheeks. He took them in his own.

"*These*. These hands. They aren't so scary anymore."

"Then why not go? What do you have to lose?"

"Absolutely nothing. I have nothing to lose."

"Yeah, so what's the problem?"

Danny let go of her hands and walked away.

*   *   *

I don't want your half-hearted love
Don't want your instant picture life
I don't want your cardboard ideals
I don't want your lies

You can take my love
Put it between your thighs
But it don't change a thing
It don't make it right

I guess I'm not the man I used to be
No, I probably never was
But if you want you can try and change me
You can play me like a marionette
Can treat me as some sort of toy
How would you like that?

But when your hands get tired
And when the show is over
Will you be so kind as to cut the wires?

Well I'm just a bit player
Scenery with no lines
You can charge admission
While I silently die

*   *   *

"Hello Daibhead, can I get you something?"

"No t'anks, Mr. Abramov. Is Natalya 'round?"

"No, sorry, I don't know where she is today."

"Well, if she comes in, let her know I was lookin' fer."

"I will do that."

"T'anks, Mr. Abramov."

"See you another time, Daibhead."

*   *   *

Meet me at the sands
Barefoot
Pants rolled up to your knees
Oh, meet with me
Meet with me
Meet with me

Meet me at the beach
Low tide
Go walking in the sea
Oh, meet with me
Meet with me
Meet with me

Meet me at sunset
Silent
Take you two-step dancing
Oh, meet with me
Meet with me
Meet with me

*   *   *

"Fin, don't get me wrong."

Sorely tried to fix the look of disgust on his best mate's face.

"Get ya wrong? Get ya wrong? How the fuck could I get ya
right? Ya make it sound as I'm an axe murderer."

A frightful, angry, stick of a man, Fintan Larkin was. An axe
murderer, he was not.

"No, no. Fintan, I'm jus' sayin' maybe ya should lay off the drink
fer a bit. Try an' behave now an' then. Moira-"

"Fuck Moira. D'ya t'ink I give a damn what Moira t'inks me?"

"She's jus' worried that ya drink too much an' it might rub off on me."

"Ridiculous."

Sorley O'Mara was struggling to find a way to balance the instructions from his girlfriend with the unusual specimen sitting next to him that rarely accepted instruction.

"Remember last week?"

"What about it?"

"Wakin' up in an alleyway is hardly normal."

"I didn't invite ya ta join me."

"I wasn't gonna go home ta her like that."

"She wouldn't like it."

"No she wouldn't."

A grown man, in most ways, even if lacking in others, Fin was not enjoying being treated as if he were a child. Passing out in an alleyway was a perfectly normal way to end an evening, even if that evening was a Monday. Until recently, Sorley himself had often encouraged these antics. These were two grown men who happened to enjoy drinking a fair bit and passing out in alleyways when it suited them. How dare a woman, especially one Sorley had just met, how dare she tell them how to behave. It was unacceptable.

"Look at yerself, Sorley, yer a grown man. Being pushed 'round by a wee woman ain't how it's s'posed ta be."

"How would ya know? You've never taken the time ta be with a woman longer than one night."

"Say that like it's a flaw. Yer jus' a fat fuck who's happy some broad likes his fat ass enough ta see him again. Yer willin' ta make her happy cuz ya can't do no better."

"Fin, I'm serious, I can't be 'round ya if ya talk 'bout her like that. I can't be 'round ya if yer always an asshole. I like ya, guy, but yer a real prick."

Larkin was surprised with how firm his fat, slobby friend was on the issue. He must really like that broad. Either that, or he was really under her thumb.

"Fine, fine. I'll keep it t'a minimum."

"An' the drink?"

"Yer not talkin' givin' it up altogether, are ya?"

"No, not entirely, but a couple pints 'stead twenty."

"Yeah, I can do that."

"Good, good. I don't t'ink Moira'll mind I have a couple pints with ya."

"An' Niall?"

"Don't get me started on her opinion Niall Dugan."

"Oh, I see, that's the way it is."

"Yeah, t'ink so."

"Fuckin' hell, mate. She's got ya hard."

"It's fer my own good. Hardly know any better."

"You've got that right. Yer a suggestible fuck aren't ya?"

"D'ya mean?"

"Nevermind."

Fintan laughed a little to himself and remembered the time that he got Sorley to moon the Gardaí.

15.
a lot of leaving

Well this old orphaned isle
It can't take much more
Since Daddy's gone to the ocean
And Mama's gone to the floor

Well our oldest brother, Charlie
In Reading he works twelve hours a day
But if you'd ask me what his job is
I couldn't for the life of me say

The next brother, Malcolm
He's a real good lookin' man
Spends his time playin' cards in Blackpool
And he's never won a hand

Our oldest sister, Mary
Oh, she met a sweet talkin' Yid
Now she's living on the Kibbutz
Taking care of her seven kids

Pretty little Gloria
Oh, we had so many hopes
She walks the streets of Camden
Trying to score some dope

Oh, come home
The house ain't the same without Papa
But we're doing okay
Oh, come home

*   *   *

Tressa sat in the empty den, the vacant shelves occupied with distant memories. She breathed in a deep waft of air. His cologne still lingered in the wallpaper. Fuck him. Forty years. Forty *fucking* years.

What a child she had been. Swept away by the romantic poet. Swept away by his words. Words. Nothing, but words.

"Someday, you'll see, Tressa, I'll be famous."

Some fame. Someday. That was a long time ago. Liam Bradigan wasn't the second coming of George Bernard Shaw. His words gathered on yellow legal pads.

"One day, I'll afford a typewriter, I'll type these up, just like a real book, and it'll be great."

They just filled boxes. Boxes upon boxes. Boxes that left when he did. Oddly, she found herself missing those boxes. When Liam was at work she used to peek at them. She'd find herself reading his unfinished poems. She had become an expert at reading his chicken-scratch.

"Should have been a doctor, they say."

A doctor, no. A clerk, yes. A clerk at the town hall. The poet she met, the one with the wavy uncontrollable hair, cut it short, worked a straight job.

"You miss it? I thought you'd like it this way?"

No, no, no. She could have married Bobby McNamara, her parents' choice. He moved to Dublin, held a job with the agriculture department, rose quite high. No, she loved that Bradigan boy, *the wild one*, the one who wasn't going to sell out.

"There's always the evenings, love. I can write then. Lots of writers hold day jobs."

He wanted to be the next Yeats, or Synge, or even Joyce, on occasion, if he was feeling ambitious.

"Next summer, the Aran Islands. We'll live like proper Irish folk."

They stayed in Leinster. Liam quickly gave up his Gaelic lessons.
The Aran Islands disappeared into the fog.

*   *   *

We can start
Innocent enough
Taking walks in the park
And feeding birds

We can start
Slowly enough
Letting it build up
Until it erupts

We can start
Trusting enough
Sharing hopes and dreams
And memories

We can start
Wildly enough
In Stephen's Green
Walking on the grass

We can start
Lovely enough
Go back to my place
Just off of Grafton

In the end
Let me know
If you're going to break me
If you're going to leave

And I'll begin wailing
You can hear me scream

No, don't leave

In the end
It's just a whisper
It quivers off my lips
And sends shivers
Down my neck

*   *   *

"Why am I here?"

"You 'preciate watchin' me serve pints ta middle-aged men?"

"Funny, Marlene, funny. But you know what I mean."

"Somet'in' wrong?"

"Danny."

"What's wrong with Danny?"

"What's right with that boy? I come back to town, I throw myself
all over him and I ask him to run away with me and he's
hesitant."

"Ya t'ink tha's an issue?"

"Any man in his right mind would want to leave here with me.
Am I right, fellas?"

The three gentlemen at the bar nodded in agreement. They'd
throw away their wives to run away with a young thing like
Saraid Doran.

"You see?"

"Very impressive, Sara. But, have ya t'ought 'bout why Danny
might be hesitant?"

"The past."

"Yes."

"But that's in the past. He should be over it. I'm long over it."

"These t'ings linger. T'was hard fer'm."

"Are you saying it wasn't hard for me?"

"Well, ya were the one who left."

"And that's easy? Marla, I had to leave all my friends, my town, my everything and go. It wasn't easy."

"An' Danny?"

"And Danny didn't have to go. He stayed. He got to keep everything. My friends. My town. My everything. He got to keep it all."

"Except his everythin'."

"Oh."

"You left everythin' that was important ta ya. Ya left with everythin' that was important ta him."

"Feck. I've been a real bitch, haven't I?"

"I don't t'ink ya meant ta."

"No, I didn't. That's the problem. I didn't think. Daniél's been sitting here for two years and I didn't think about what he was going through."

"There ya go. Now yer onta somet'in'."

"Marla, what should I do? Was it wrong for me to come back? Am I just stirring up emotions that don't need to be stirred?"

"I can't say, love, I dunno."

"This is a big mistake."

"Don't be rash. You an' Danny have been gettin' 'long well other than this one incident. Give'm some time. Let him say his peace. He deserves that."

"Yeah, he does. He really is a fantastic man."

"Far too few Danny Doyles out there. If ya don't treat him right this time I may jump him myself."

"Your love life as rotten as mine, Marla?"

"If I only had an ex ta try an' win back. I t'ink I need a boyfriend first. Then I can lose him an' try again. Yer in a different league than me, Saraid."

"You're a pretty girl, I'm surprised."

"There ain't an abundance, quality fellas 'round here, as ya can tell."

"Anybody you fancy?"

"There's one fella. He comes in here occasionally with his brother. Farrell's the name. The younger one."

"Nic Farrell? He's kinda cute, I guess. In a weird sort of way."

"Ya t'ink he's weird?"

"I dunno, I haven't really seen much of him since I've been back but he always seems so preoccupied with himself. Always there, physically that is, but absent, up top."

"He's an artist. He must have a million t'oughts goin' on."

"Oh, I've seen his art. It's okay. Not Jack Yeats, but okay, for here anyways."

"I've never actually seen anyt'in' he's painted."

"Well, there is your first date; ask him to show you some art. His self-absorbed self would love that."

"I don't t'ink he's self-absorbed. But, then again he's never noticed me at all. But, that's cuz I don't t'ink I'm even his type. He's probably into cellists or activists or that sort. Not a barmaid."

"Interesting, Marla has herself a crush. Well I'll be on the lookout for Mr. Farrell, *the younger*, and see if he is indeed dating a cello-playing activist or if he is single and looking for an attractive bar-maiden to run away with to some art exhibit in Prague, or more likely in his case, *Belfast*."

*   *   *

"Well, hello Daibhead, can I fetch you something?"

"No, t'anks, Mrs. Abramov. Is Natalya 'round?"

"No, sorry, love, I don't know where she is today. I hope she
hasn't run off to the city-"

"Umm, well, if she comes in, or if ya see her at home, let her
know I came lookin' fer."

"Yes, I can do that, Daibhead."

"T'anks, Mrs. Abramov."

"Not a problem, Daibhead. No, nothing's a problem."

*   *   *

"Didya talk ta Fintan an' Niall?"

"Yes. No. Well, I talked ta Fin."

"An' Niall?"

"Didn't show up."

"He didn't show up?"

"No."

"Ya called him?"

"Yeah, yeah, I rang him up an' I invited him fer a pint at the pub.
Jus' like ya said I should. He said he'd be over. He never
came. I rang him from the pub an' he wasn't home. I
thought he must be on his way. He never came."

"But ya talked ta Fintan?"

"Yes, Moira. I talked ta Fin."

"And?"

"An' he said he's willin' tone it down 'round me."

"Good. Ya know I only want what's best fer ya."

"He's my best friend."

"I know, that's why it's important ya can still be 'round him. I'm
glad ta hear he's willin' put in effort."

"He will."

"Good. Now we jus' need t'ave a word with that Dugan

character."

"Well, he can ring me up. I'm not goin' through that effort again. I walked all the way down ta pub an' back fer not'in'."

"Not'in'?"

"Well, I may have had a pint."

"Yer breath smells like ya had more than one."

"T'was a strong one."

"Sorley, f'we're t'ave a serious adult relationship ya need ta be completely honest with me."

"Okay, so I had three pints. I waited a long time fer Niall ta not show."

"I don't have a problem with ya havin' three pints, what I have a problem with is ya tellin' me y'only had one. A strong one, at that."

"I'm sorry love, t'won't happen again."

"Good pet, I jus' want us ta be happy."

"I'm happy."

"Good. Though that might jus' be that strong pint ya drank."

"No, truth. I'm really happy with ya."

"Good, I'm almost there with ya too."

16.
mark my words

You had left. I remember it well. There was a small box in my pocket. You know the one. I had wanted to open it so badly, but you beat me to the moment, and twisted it into something so very different, so now that day will forever be etched in my mind for all the wrong reasons. The sixteenth of June was our anniversary. It was when I wanted to ask you the most important question a man could ever ask. Instead, you had to say goodbye, there'd be no other words to leave your mouth, then. Certainly not 'yes'. I was shattered, like a crystal figurine, though I may not look like it now; there are a million cracks in me, held together by glue.

It's amazing, though, what time, and hindsight, and the long road in between events can do. The change I experienced between then and now. I think we can both appreciate the necessity, as harsh it might have felt at the time, that you and I could no longer be entwined. It had run its course. I'd stay up late and wonder about the what-ifs and the maybes and know that there had to be separation between us, even though it was the last thing I wanted. But you pushed it upon me, so I didn't have a choice. For the sake of carving our own lives we couldn't be together. I understand, finally. Even though, seeing you here makes me wonder whether, perhaps, it's different now. We're different now. That's the point, I think. We couldn't be some sort of pairing of halflings, we needed to be whole before we could come together right. Are you whole now?

*   *   *

"Mr. Shannon. How nice of you to come in. I was just on my way over to drop off the *Independent*."

"Not necessary taday, I'll take it myself."

"Anything else for you?"

"No, Sergei, I don't t'ink I need anythin' else. That's not the reason for my stoppin' by, though."

"No?"

"No. Eoghan tells me that you've sent Maksim away."

"Yes, to Dublin. He's living there with a friend. Found a job at a restaurant, I believe."

"I am t'understand that ya told him not come back."

"Not exactly. I told him to become a man first."

"Oh, I see. 'Become a man'. I see."

"Do you not approve, Mr. Shannon?"

"It's a very uncommon t'ing ta do."

"No, that is right, uncommon, yes, but strong."

"Very *traditional*."

"Traditional?"

"Yes, in many cultures, when a boy became a certain age, his family would abandon him in the wild. He'd have ta survive, hunt, scavenge, an' find his way back home. A rite'f passage."

"Yes! This is the idea."

"D'ya not t'ink Maksim has already passed those tests?"

"No."

"He's livin' on his own. He's found a job. You've made yer point."

"When he is a man he can come home."

"Sergei, when he becomes a man, there will be no more home."

"Sir?"

"Grown men don't come home. They have their own homes. When it's time. Maksim is old enough take care'f himself; he's proven that. But now is not the time. He's still in university. Let the biggest stress in his life be his exams. He'll have plenty'f time t'worry about everyt'in' else when he's yer age. An' then, once he's mine, he'll have no worries t'all."

"Mr. Shannon, I appreciate your words, but I think I know what is best for my son."

"Did yer father do this ta you, Sergei?"

"No."

"An' how did ya turn out?"

"I'd like to think I am a good man."

"So why wouldn't Maksim?"

"I don't like the path he is on. He shirks his responsibilities. His commitments don't matter to him."

"I'd say his studies matter ta him."

"Yes, but what does all that knowledge do for him? History does not pay the bills. I have to work long shifts here to provide for my family. He can't understand that. He's not willing to work his shifts when he is asked to."

"Maybe he doesn't wanna."

"This I know, Mr. Shannon, this I know."

"Is that a bad thing, Sergei?"

"One day, I would have liked to give the store to him."

"Is it wrong fer'm t'want better fer'mself? Don't begrudge the boy. Let him come home. Put the roof o'er his head. Give'm that gift, now, not the store later."

"I can't. I made a point to him. I must stick with it."

"That's a very stubborn attitude."

"If I act weak, he'll think it's okay to be weak as a man."

"Loving yer son ain't weak. It's prolly the strongest t'ing ya could do."

"Where did you learn to love Eoghan the way you do? Your father?"

"Yes, Sergei. I'm afraid I did learn t'love my son from my father. Though the lessons he taught me were far from perfect, I could use them as a jumping off point. My father was a good man. But he was hardly a good dad. I'm scared ta t'ink that ya remind me somewhat him."

*   *   *

"Moira wants us ta do what?"

"She wants us ta behave 'round Sorley."

"That's fuckin' bullshit, that is."

"I know."

Fintan scraped the white powder off his nostrils.

"Ya know what Sorley's problem is?"

"What?"

"He's so enamoured with the *thought'f love,* that he's deluded
himself inta t'inkin' he's *in love.* He can't stop himself. He'll
do anyt'in' fer this broad."

Niall lined up another rail on the kitchen counter.

"Exactly. He's so fuckin' fat th'any woman that'll lay him is
bound ta be the love 'f'his life."

"It's crazy. She sounds like a psycho bitch."

"She seemed normal 'nuff when we met her, well, other than her
face bein' all scrunched up at everyt'in' we said."

"How dare she? She's got the ugliest accent. It made my ears
bleed, I swear. I don't know what driftwood she floated in
on, but her voice is brutal."

"I know, an' t'ink she works in a bank. What sort reputable
financial institution would hire that woman? T'wouldn't
surprise me she was raised by pirates."

Niall put his nose to the counter and swiftly made the blow
disappear with one suck.

"What the hell does she mean, 'behave'?"

"I haven't got a clue."

"What a bitch."

"Totally. Sorley's got it bad."

"Poor lad."

*   *   *

Drag me down
Through the mud
You might as well
I've been choking
On dirt for so long

Respectable
Not so long ago
You might remember
What I once was
Yesterday

I'm singing for change
Belting out my lungs
To buy some smokes
And a dram
Anything to warm me

Replaceable
There's a dozen
Guys like me
Out there

Take your pick
Take your pick
Take your pick
And go

*   *   *

"Hello, Alan. How are you?"

"Umm, well, t'anks."

"That's nice."

"Yes, it is."

Alan's hands wrung themselves over repeatedly.

"Saraid, first 'f all, I'd like ta say I'm sorry."

"Sorry for what?"

His face blushed.

"Fer what happened, ya know, th'other week."

"You don't need to. I guess you felt overwhelmed with life."

"No, well, yes. But what I meant was I am sorry fer askin' y'out right before *that*. I don't want ya t'ink I did it 'cuz ya said no."

"Oh."

"'Cuz it had not'in' really ta do with that."

"Oh."

"Yeah, I jus' wanna be clear that I didn't try ta drown myself because ya rejected me."

"Why did you? If you don't mind me asking."

"That don't matter. I jus' want ya ta know it wasn't 'cuzza ya."

"Oh, alright. Thank you, I guess."

17.
sometimes, truth can hurt

No, I don't give a damn
About your old man
I don't give a damn
About you and him

*   *   *

"Hi Daibhead."

"Natalya, I've been lookin' all over for ya."

"I know."

"Have ya been hidin' from me?"

"I have."

"Why?"

"What do you want from me, Daibhead?"

"I thought we were friends."

"Friends? We're not friends, Daibhead, not at all. Friends are the people you hang out with, get drunk with, go see a fucking movie. Whatever. Friends are the people that are there for you through thick and thin and don't give a fuck. We're not friends."

Daibhead Shannon's face displayed that common look of confusion, befuddlement, and pure fear that every teenage boy (or even grown men, for that matter) displays when confronted by an attractive girl whose switch has been officially changed from 'docile' to 'attack crazy bitch' mode.

"Where's this all comin' from? We do those t'ings."

"Yeah, we do those things *now*. Why didn't we ever do those things before?"

"Before?"

"Yeah, why didn't we do those things before Ánna left?"

"I dunno."

"You sure don't. I'm not somebody's ragdoll to be tossed around when they feel like it."

"I dunno what ta say."

Eighteen-year-old Daibh Shannon was on a collision course towards learning what buttons you do not push with women.

"Say something. *Anything*. I don't want to be your buddy when your girlfriend is out of town only to be thrown to the side when she comes back. Real friends don't do that."

"I'm sorry."

"I don't want that. Not at all. Why do you want to be around me so much? Where're your mates? Go hang out with them."

"I like ya, Nat, sorry I wanted ta be yer friend."

"No, I'm sorry, Daibhead, because I really like you, and I can't be just your friend."

"Why not?"

I'm not sure if Daibhead was lying or completely bewildered by the situation.

"That's not what I want. I don't need another person to gab to or to go shopping with. I'm not looking for that."

"Nat, I-"

"I know."

"I love Ánna."

"I know."

"I t'ought we could be friends."

"That's too hard for me. I don't know what you want. I don't know what you expect. I don't like being second fiddle and I don't want to hear a word about how much you miss her.

I don't want to be a shoulder to cry on. That's not me. I want to be the girl that you tell your other friends that you miss and that you want to be with."

"I'm sorry, tha's jus' not the case."

"There must be some reason why you've gone through all this effort just to track me down."

"Because yer my friend, not'in' more, not'in' less. I take my friendships seriously. I wanted ta hang out with ya. I want ta hang out with ya. Yer cool, I like ya, you get me. There doesn't have ta be anyt'in' more than that."

"But there is. I'm not going to be some sort of proxy girlfriend, filling in the void while she's away. I'm not."

"I'm not askin' ya."

"You are."

"Well, I'm sorry ta hear that ya can't be more mature 'bout it. There doesn't have ta be anyt'in' more than that. I jus' wanna be yer friend."

"You lie, Daibhead, I know you do. Every guy wants more than just friends. You all want more."

"No. That's not true."

"It is. Guys and girls can't just be friends. There is always some level of sexual tension. Admit it."

"That's not always the case."

"It is right now, isn't it?"

"You don't need ta bring this up."

"Admit it, Daibh, you're attracted to me."

"Yer an attractive girl."

"Don't describe me; tell me what you think, what you feel."

"Yes, I am attracted ta you."

"So can't you see how hard it must be to just be friends?"

"There are lots 'f'attractive people, that is people I am attracted to, that I somehow manage ta control myself 'round jus' fine."

"I don't want you to have to 'control yourself' around me. Those
feelings mean something. You shouldn't bottle yourself up
like that. It's not healthy."

"Natalya, don't push me like this. Friends don't do that. Why
can't ya trust that I love Ánna an' jus' leave it at that? Why
can't ya support me an' not try tempt me?"

"Because you don't need to be pushed. You're already tempted.
You don't go searching for your other mates like this, do
you?"

"Yer bad fer me."

"I am, am I?"

"You are."

"Well, how about you spend some time with yourself and come
find me when you figure I'm good for you?"

*　　*　　*

"How are ya, Tress?"

"Fine, Eoghan, t'anks."

"Are ya really?"

Tressa looked her son-in-law in the eyes and tears formed.

"I got a letter from Liam."

"Oh."

"He's enjoyin' himself."

"Really, how are you?"

"Obviously, not enjoyin' myself. He says he's gettin' married
there. Found some young girl."

"I'm sorry, Tress."

"Oh, s'alright. I already knew we were done when he first left.
He went on 'bout his lost dreams an' the life he was sick of.

All this. Me, here, everyt'in'. When the papers came I signed them right away. T'was almost routine. Jus' a natural motion ta sign my name, cross the 't', dot the 'i', all that. Not emotional. T'was jus' another form."

"But this is different."

"T'is. It's one t'ing ta say goodbye t'a man you've loved forever. It's another t'ing ta hear from him that his new life is so much better all'f'a sudden. Like that's all it takes. As everyt'in' we built over these years was jus' a waste, an' the instant he meets some teenage whore in Asia his whole life has been given meanin'."

"Ya goin' ta be alright?"

"I always manage. I jus' never t'ought this is what my life would become. Jus' bein' 'alright'. I guess I had put my expectations a little higher."

"I t'ink we all do."

Put on your happy face and go to town, go round your errands, the same old routine as before, go, go, go. And, when you've gone you can return to home, crawl into your bed and let the light turn off. When it's good and dark and you're all alone, let the tears roll down your cheeks. Let it all out, tomorrow you must put on your happy face again and go to town, go round your errands, the same old routine.

"Eoghan, yer a good man, listenin' t'old lady's troubles."

"Yer family, Tressa."

"T'anks. That means a lot. I don't have many people ta lean on these days."

"Ya can never lean too hard."

"T'ank you."

*   *   *

"Hi Marla, I'll have a pint."

Marlene Cullen turned to the bar to see the face of Mícheál Farrell.

"Hullo Mícheál, how are ya?"

"Been better, thanks."

"Oh yeah? Tough day?"

"Tough week. Tough month."

"Sorry ta hear that."

"It's alright, it's not breaking news or anything."

"Wanna talk 'bout it?"

"No, I'd rather not, thanks."

"Sorry, anyt'in' else ya wanna talk 'bout?"

"Not especially."

"How's yer brother?"

"Nic? He's fine, I guess."

"Haven't seen him 'round here lately, is all."

If a woman had ever been more obvious with her affection, I cannot say.

"I dunno, he's probably busy with his art. Been painting a lot."

"Has he? Anyt'in' good?"

"No, I dunno, haven't seen anything."

"I'd really like ta see summa his art sometime."

"Could we stop talking about Nic? I'm really not in the mood."

"Sorry, I didn't know that was a sore subject, I was jus' askin' how he was."

"Listen, the last thing I want to talk about is my brother's art. Why can't you just be a barmaid and serve me my pint and leave me alone?"

136

Marla placed the pint in front of Mícheál and walked away. His attitude was hardly friendly. She didn't need to hear that sort of shit. Several minutes passed and Mícheál had finished his drink when he sighed and spoke again.

"I'm sorry, Marlene. I didn't mean to be so short."

Marla was washing glasses and had her back to him. She spoke over her shoulder to him while continuing her task.

"I'm sorry I asked anyt'in'."

"Don't be like that."

"Jus' a barmaid. Jus' washin' glasses, servin' pints, who cares what I have t'ask?"

"I'm sorry."

"Ya should be."

"Well, I am."

"I jus' wanted t'ask 'bout yer brother, I t'ought you'd be happy talk about him. I always t'ought you were close."

"We are. What do you want to know? Wait - why all these questions about him?"

Mícheál had finally started to clue in. If I haven't mentioned it to you before, indeed, now is as good a time as any to mention that we men are the slower gender.

"I dunno."

"Yes, you do. You've never once asked me about him before. What's going on?"

"D'ya promise ta keep a secret?"

"No."

"Fine, I'll tell y'anyways."

"Well, what is it?"

"I fancy yer brother."

"Nicolás?"

"D'ya have any others?"

"Seriously? You have a thing for Nicolás? Where'd that come out of?"

"I jus' do, okay?"

"I'd never have thought him to be your type."

"What type is that, then?"

"I don't know. Just not him."

"An' why not him?"

"I don't know. I've just never figured you to be into guys that were, you know, like him."

"Artistic? Intelligent? Good-looking? No, I couldn't imagine me bein' inta someone *like that.*"

"You've just never struck me as someone who would date Nic."

"What's wrong with me?"

"Oh, nothing. I just didn't think you'd be his type."

"His type? My type? All these types! Why can't two people jus' be together? Do we need types?"

"Certain people match up with other certain people. I just never figured for you matching up with Nic."

Stupid, stupid, Mícheál.

"Why? Because I'm not educated enough?"

"Maybe."

"For a butcher ya sure are a snob."

"I went to architectural school."

"Yer still a butcher."

Way back then, oh, so long ago
I was a man without a name
I did not have anything to offer
But you loved me all the same
Our love grew ever so quick
From sweet summer romance
To flourishing relationship
Built on a young boy's advance

Oh, how could you refuse?

Way back then, not so long ago
You were a girl, oh, so pretty
I remember the first day we kissed
You came skippin' to greet me
I could barely believe it
Outstretched arms around my back
You made your affection known
Subtlety was never your tact

Oh, how could I refuse?

Oh, please, blame the heat
I can't even bother to eat
I think I've lost twenty pounds
And my phone don't make a sound

I'm still waiting

Oh, how could I,
Oh, how could I,
Ever lose?

The absence grows, and it grows
And the heart, well, it knows
There ain't nothing it can do
I could run away for good
Won't fix it, nothing ever could

I'm just left here, oh, without you

Without you

18.
the cold shoulder

"I can't believe that Fintan Larkin."

"What now, love?"

"I saw him stumblin' 'long High Street when I was shoppin', drunk off his ass, bottle in hand."

"Oh."

"'Oh'? That's it?"

"Well, it isn't too surprisin'."

"It's not surprisin' see a grown man, drunk off his ass on High Street at eleven in the mornin'?"

Sorley really didn't think too hard about Moira's investigative questioning. There had been many mornings, on a regular basis, when he had joined Fin and Niall in sitting on High Street, bottles in hand.

"No, it's quite common."

"Sure, it may be 'common' with yer degenerate friends but if ya want ta do somet'in' with yer life ya'd better steer clear that sort."

"What's the big deal?"

"What if it had been you, Sorley?"

"I'd say the day had started off quite nice."

"Seriously."

Moira didn't catch, or chose to ignore, that her boyfriend had been quite serious.

"Oh, I dunno, give him a break, he's enjoyin' himself."

"Goin' ta pub an' drinkin' is one t'ing. He's out there drinkin' his life away. He's a mess. I don't want ya ta fall inta that."

"Moira, please. I'm not gonna be runnin' through the streets drunk off my ass at eleven in the mornin'."

Anymore, anyways, he thought.

"Ya better not be. There's so much more ta life than that."
"I know, I know."

Sorley wondered if maybe Moira could provide him with a list, or something, of things that would be both enjoyable and approved behaviour.

"What has he got in his head that makes him so stupid?"
"I t'ink that's the problem, he hasn't got a t'ing."

Sorley lied. He knew that Fintan Larkin was actually a very intelligent person. He just happened to suffer from a lack of application. Fin had figured out a method of calculating probabilities that allowed him to have an overall winning record at sports gambling. He just couldn't be bothered to make the bets.

"Is he really such a good person ta be around?"
"He's my best friend."

Who else was he going to pick? Niall Dugan?

"He's no good, Sorley, I've warned ya."
"He's my best friend."
"Ya can't be 'round him. He's like a tickin' bomb."
"He's harmless. He wouldn't harm a fly."
"Ya don't know that. I've had a bad feelin' 'bout him forever. He's jus' pure trouble, Sor. Ya don't need that."
"He's my best friend."

"Make new friends. Meet normal people. People with jobs. People with lives that don't revolve 'round a pint here, a line there."

"Boring people?"

"Sorley."

"I'm sorry, but he's been my mate fer a very long time."

"Can ya jus' stay clear him fer yer own sake?"

"Moira."

"Ya know it's a bad idea bein' 'round him. He jus' gets ya inta situations any sane person would stay clear."

"It's hard ta stop bein' 'round him. He's my best friend. I've known him forever."

"When ya were younger did ya ever wear diapers?"

"Yes, course, when I was an baby."

"What didya do when ya had diapers?"

"I shat myself."

"Right. Now did ya get ta the point where ya realised that shittin' yer pants was a bad idea?"

"Well no, not on my own, eventually my parents decided I was old 'nuff ta use the toilet."

"An' once ya got used ta the toilet have ya ever felt the need ta shit yer pants again?"

"No, course not."

"D'ya see where I am goin' with this?"

"No, not exactly."

"I'm sayin' it's time ta grow up. Fintan is like shittin' yer pants. It was fun when yer young an' don't know any better, but yer not young nomore an' it's jus' ridiculous fer ya t'act like him an' t'ink it's okay."

"Okay, I get it. It's time ta grow up."

"Well that means it's time ta start toilet training. Ya can't keep hangin' 'round Fintan Larkin. It's time ta move on."

"Alright. I'll try."

"Ya know it's fer yer own good."

"Yeh, I guess."

*   *   *

I'm not surprised
You've ended up here
To face the facts
And settle old scores
We can finally agree on
Who loved who more

*   *   *

Danny was still reeling. What a horrible night. He felt gutted.

"Here's ta Saraid Doran, the prettiest girl in Leinster!"

The crowd's cheers filled his head. He couldn't believe how she had acted. What nerve.

"Thanks boys, the highest bidder will receive a date with me which will include dinner and a movie, for sure, and maybe, if you're lucky, a little pecking. Not too much, though."

He was right there. She saw him. She *knew*. How could she act that way? Did she mean any of it? How could she act that way?

"Danny, don't be so stiff, it's all for charity."

Charity. Of course. How could he forget that? Sara was a sucker for that stuff. Raising money for one thing or another. Still, she could have shown some restraint.

"Come on, boys, let's get out your pocketbooks. I'm single and looking for an evening out, or in, for charity."

What was she saying? Did she mean any of it? Single? What had happened? Wasn't she just professing her love for him? How could she do that?

"Sara, what do you think of our winner here?"
"Oh, he looks lovely. I can't wait."

Daniél felt sick. He slunk out the backdoor of the pub without anyone noticing. He hadn't bothered to leave a note or say a thing to Eoghan. This was all too much.

The phone rang.

"Hello?"

"Danny. It's me, where'd you take off? Eoghan was worried."

"Oh, Eoghan was worried, was he? Thanks."

"Is there something wrong?"

He lay on his bed with the receiver next to his ear on the pillow. His eyes were closed but reddening on the inside.

"Danny?"

"What?"

"Is there something wrong?"

"I have to go, Saraid."

He placed the receiver back on its stand, rolled over and let his face melt into the pillow.

*   *   *

I sat for hours, days on end, waiting to hear from you. I heard nothing. I'd go off, and try and fill a day with activities, busyness, anything to keep my mind off of you. Nothing worked. Do you understand the power that a woman loved possesses? The man who loves her is drawn into her, pulled into a foreboding spell, *the siren song*, do you understand? We're porcelain figurines in your hands, men, and you women can willfully destroy us with a carefree toss. It's not intended; no, I highly doubt that. It's the opposite, and that is what hurts the most. We can take the hits when they are expected. From our enemies, rivals, superiors, et cetera. We can be bombarded with hurtful words or actions from *out there* until we are oblivious to their existence. What hurts the most is when the blows come from inside our inner circle, from those we've let into our vulnerability. A man can be a powerful being. He can be a raw physical or intellectual brute, intimidated by no man. He can also be a raw nerve, exposed to feel the sharpest pain from the closest source.

19.
rain in june

"How are ya, Maks? It's been awhile."

"It has, Danny, I've missed ya, pal."

"How's Dublin?"

"Same old. Here?"

"Same old."

"Ya seen my dad?"

"Occasionally, yeah, I don't really venture much across the street."

"No, you were never much for exercise."

"Can't be bothered."

Danny kept a weight set at his house.

"How's Sara?"

"Don't get me started."

"Really?"

"Yeah, really."

"Sorry I asked."

"It's okay. I just don't know what to do. I don't know why she is here, what she wants, why she acts the way she does, how I am supposed to take it all in."

"What do ya figure she wants?"

"She says she wants me."

"Well that's simple enough."

"But it seems like half the time she wants me and the other half of the time she is flirting with every man in town."

"Shit. Why'd she do that?"

"I'd hope it's to grab my attention."

"And it's obviously worked."

"It has. I do like her. We get on well. But there's always this piercing feeling in the back of my head telling me to run like hell away from her."

"That can't be good."

"No, probably. But it is such an intense feeling that you know it's something."

"Like what?"

"Well, like love, maybe."

"Love makes you want to run like hell?"

"No, not exactly. What I mean is that when I am around her I get this piercing feeling, it's like an intense sharpness that is almost smacking me across the head. It's like warning me that things are too good to be true and that I need to wake up, run away and hide."

"And that's love?"

"Sure, it's so frightening that this person has the potential to bring you every sort of happiness you've ever wanted and yet at the same time the potential to deny you exactly that."

"That is scary."

"So the smack at the back of the head is telling me to run, forget her, be alone and miserable and move on."

"That doesn't sound much better."

"No, exactly. Do I want to be miserable and alone, knowing that I had the chance at happiness but walked away? Or do I want to risk everything and possibly end off extremely miserable and alone, knowing that all chance of happiness has been stolen from me?"

Maksim looked at the man and saw a frightened boy, unwilling to leave his house, for fear of the world outside. No chance of being harmed. But, also no chance of fulfillment.

"There's still the chance that you get the girl, you become extremely happy and avoid those horrible conclusions."

"Yeah, that's what I obviously want. But there's always that small amount of fear."

That small, *gigantic* amount of fear.

"That she could destroy you?"

"Yeah, for sure."

"Women are scary."

"Yeah."

"So what do you do, Danny Doyle?"

"I don't know. I'm sitting at a giant fork in the road and I have to decide. I can't go much longer floating, waiting to find out. I'll have to commit to a one-way path and let fate decide."

"Ecstatic joy and happiness or eternal solitude and sorrow."

"Yeah, something along those lines."

"That's a lot of pressure to put on yerself."

"That's a lot of pressure to put on Saraid Doran."

"Does she realise that she means that much to you?"

"I don't know half the things that she realises. She's a complete mystery."

"Aren't they all?"

"No, not like her. That's why she scares me so much."

*　　*　　*

Mícheál rapped on the door. He couldn't wait for his brother to answer.

"Nicolás? You home?"

He tried opening the door. It was locked.

"Nicolás, come on, open up."

He was still standing there, waiting.

"Artists."

*   *   *

Hands in pockets
Shoulders shrugged
Eyes half open
That's your love

I don't know what to say
To make things right
I don't know what to say
To win this fight
I don't know anything at all

Lacklustre hearts breed romance
The kind in back seats
The kind that don't last
The kind that goes with steam

I don't know what to say
To make things right
I don't know what to say
To win this fight
I don't know anything at all

I thought I did

I thought I did
I thought I did with you
Everything in this world
Could fail me but you

I guess I was wrong

*   *   *

Alan sat in his stark flat. The bare walls taunting him.

"What a fine mess we have here, Mr. Brennan."

His thoughts rushed through his brain while his body was comatose, listless, a corpse.

"What a fine mess, indeed."

Memories of places been and things seen bombarded his soul.

"Alan, what do you think of it here?"
"It's lovely, Mummy, lovely."
"Oh good. We'll be moving here soon, I'm glad you like it."
"Moving here?"
"Why yes, dear, Mr. Flannigan wants us to move here with him."

Alan Brennan was a skeleton that had long lost his skin.

"Brennan, you suck."
"Alan, you're fired."
"Mr. Brennan, would you please come sit at the front."
"Hey Brennan, give me yer money."
"I'm sorry, Alan, but I don't feel the same way."
"Queer."
"Loser."
"You'll never amount to anything, Alan."

There was never a single moment that could define him. Well, perhaps one that summed the whole thing up. When the boulder sailed down from the bridge, rope in tow, Alan watched expectantly, until the boulder hit the water, the rope with it, and Alan was still watching.

20.
when it rains, it pours

"I'm pregnant."

A woman who had spent the majority of her life avoiding expectations, avoiding trying to get her hopes up, for fear of being thwarted was expecting.

"What?"

"I'm pregnant, Sorley."

A man who had spent the majority of his life avoiding expectations, avoiding trying to get anyone's hopes up, for fear of being unable to deliver was expecting.

"Moira."

"I'm pregnant with yer child."

"I'm speechless. I dunno what ta say."

"Sorley, yer goin' ta be a father."

*   *   *

"Eoghan, come close."

"I'm right here, Da, I am."

"The doctor paid me a visit today."

"And?"

"Eoghan, it's bad."

"Da?"

"He figures that I've only gotta few weeks, maybe a month or two at most."

"No, don't say that."

"I can't change any'f that. I'm sorry."

"Da."

"Yer a great man, Eoghan, I know you are, don't be afraid."

"I jus' dunno what I'll do."

"You'll carry on. Ya will. It's all bound ta happen at some point."

"I dunno what ta do."

"Jus' sit here with me."

"An' then what?"

Eoghan broke down. He held his father's meek hand in his. He pushed his face down into Pádraig's chest and sobbed. This was his da.

*　　*　　*

Where do the heroes go,
When the battle's done?
There're many theories out there
And I've got one

The good men fall
The great men rise
The good, mere droplets
The great, tears in God's eyes

*　　*　　*

"I've got to get out of this town before it kills me."

A town of failed realisations, a town of unmet expectations, unfulfilled dreams; this was not the town for Saraid Doran.

"Don't talk like that, Sara."

"It's all a mess. I should have left earlier. No, no, no, I should have never come back."

She paced frantically back and forth across the room.

"Why? 'Cuz ya hit a rough patch with Danny?"

"It's complicated."

Marla Cullen was sick of hearing how complicated love was. She just wanted some complications of her own. These inconsiderate people that spent every aching hour obsessing over the little details of their romances, oblivious to the outside world.

"S'leave."

"What?"

"Leave. Get outta here. Jus' go, Saraid, go. But don't ya come back never again."

"Marlene."

"Isn't that what ya want ta hear? You've threatened ta leave before. I convinced ya ta stay. I told ya ta be patient with Danny. A rough patch is all it takes. Go, leave, jus' go."

"You don't understand anything, Marla!"

"I don't understand? You don't understand! Sara, ya get everybody's attention when yer 'round. You could have any man ya want. *Any* man. D'ya know what it feels like ta be second best? That's how I feel when I am 'round you. Ya complain about every t'ing that's ever an issue. Not'in' is perfect. Not'in'. D'ya understand? Do you?"

"Stop."

Sara's heart had been pressed at the epicentre.

"No, I won't stop. Daniél is amazin'. Ya know that. Why would ya leave'f t'ings get messy? Is he not worth stickin' 'round fer? If ya won't stay fer him, you'll never find nobody worth stayin' fer."

"Please, stop."

Sara wanted this all to go away, right now. She wanted to close her eyes and wake up in Geneva. No Marlene Cullen. No Daniél Doyle. Just Geneva.

"Why didya leave in the first place? What happened then? Didya have a disagreement? Did somet'in' get screwed up? Did yer perfect world crumble?"

"Marla, stop! Please, stop!"

"Daniél deserves the best. He's a great guy. He doesn't need ta be jerked 'round again. If yer goin' ta do that t'him, jus' leave now. Please, jus' go. Get lost, leave this place. Yer jus' stirrin' up a lotta anger an' hurt an' we'd all be so much better 'f'ya jus' left."

"I know. I know. I really do. It's not easy."

Berlin, Barcelona, Brussels, Budapest, Bucharest; any city that began with a 'B' would do. She'd leave right now.

"No, it's not. You'll never find easy."

"You think I don't know that? I knew exactly that when I came back! Daniél isn't easy. He's complicated. He's complex. He intimidates me. I don't know what he sees in me. I've screwed up a thousand times, Marla. I just want him to be happy. I'm done. I have to go. He can't be happy while I am here. I can't make him happy."

"Of course you can."

Every cell in her body wanted to believe what Marla said, and still Sara, in this town of disappointment, spoke of the most failed realisation she could know.

"No, I can't. No one can. *Nothing* can."

21.
it'd be a lot easier if it wasn't so hard

"I'm sorry. I was wrong."

Maksim Abramov looked at his father's blushed face. The fact that he had come into the city to say those words in person made the moment.

"It's okay. In a way, I think you were right. I needed this."

"Maksim, you are a fine boy. No, you are a fine *man*. I'm proud to call you my son."

Maks had never seen his dad so open and honest.

"Thank you, Dad."

"You're always welcome to come home."

"Thanks, I might take you up on that offer."

"Your mother would like that."

"She hasn't gone mental, has she?"

"Well, she's always been a tad off, hasn't she?"

"I won't tell her you said that."

"Thank you."

"But seriously, you wouldn't mind if I moved home?"

"No."

"That's a huge relief. Money has been really tight lately and I have exams and papers coming up, I could use the time off work."

"What?"

"Dad, you said you were proud of me."

"Okay, okay. Focus on your studies. You are welcome to move home, no strings attached."

"I really do appreciate that."

"I just want you to be happy."

"That means a lot."

*　　*　　*

Daniél, Nicolás and Mícheál sat at the end of the pier, drinking from tallboy cans of ale. The warm summer wind blew against their faces as they looked out into the endless horizon.

"Does it get any better than this?"

"I sure hope so."

Daniél said the words without consideration, and sipped from the can.

"Why so down, Danny?"

"I dunno. Is this what you thought you'd be like? You know, when you were growin' up didya think you'd turn up like this?"

"Not exactly, but I like where I'm at, maybe where I'm going."

"What about you, Mike?"

"No. No, Danny, I didn't think this was the way I'd be."

"Mikey wanted to be an astronaut when he grew up."

The three men chuckled. Mícheál took a swig of his beer and stood up.

"I had once thought that I'd go up in a rocket, the first to depart from Ireland. From some barley field, or something. Go straight up into the sky and look down from up there, and all this, all this in front of us now, would just be a tiny speck out the rocket window."

"It's true. He used to build little models of rockets. He'd paint them green. *The Irish Astronaut*."

"I doubt they'd let that happen."

"For sure, probably fall asleep at the controls."

"Passed out drunk."

"You're both terrible."

"Not as shit as you'd be as an astronaut."

"Fair play."

*   *   *

Love is a disease
And if you please
I need the cure
I'm on my knees
I'm begging please
What's the cure?

Trigger finger
My big mouth
Gets me in trouble
Gets me hooked

Poison fills my veins
What is this disease?

*   *   *

Moira woke with the warm summer breeze blowing through the open window of her bedroom. She turned over in the bed to greet her boyfriend with a playful morning peck. Sorley O'Mara was not there, though.

"Sorley? Y'in the bath?"

She leapt from the vacant bed and began investigating the various rooms in her flat, searching for her missing partner. When she returned in defeat to sit on the edge of the mattress Moira realised that half the drawers were open and items were sprawled everywhere. He had left sometime in the middle of the night without a sound, quite a feat for the large, bumbling man.

*   *   *

"I'm done, Marla, I'm done."

"Saraid, don't talk like that."

"I'm at the end of my rope. There's no point. Danny is a hopeless case."

"He's not and you know that."

"I don't know what I know anymore."

"Stay. Please, don't give up. If you leave now there's no third chance with him."

22.
silence

Daibhead sat at the postbox waiting for the carrier to bring the daily mail. He was expecting to hear something from Ánna. Anticipation had been building in him since the last letter he had sent off must have long reached her by now with plenty of time to spare for a reply.

*   *   *

"Pádraig, the headmaster spoke to me today."

"Oh."

The lanky teenager looked at his father's eyes and saw dormant wrath lurking.

"He said yer not likely ta finish."

"Did he?"

"Ya damned well know that's what he said."

"Ah."

"D'ya have anyt'in' say fer yerself?"

"No, sir."

Lochlan Shannon stood up and walked out of the room. Paddy followed.

"What d'ya want me ta say?"

"Pardon?"

"What do you want me ta say?"

"What d'ya want ta say fer yerself? Huh? You've been missing classes. When ya do show up, yer never amountin' ta not'in'. What happened, Pádraig?"

"Not'in' happened."

"Yer right, not'in'. You've done not'in' and you've become not'in'. Yer likely ta be not'in', too."

"That's a bit harsh."

"Don't tell me what harsh is."

"Y'ave no idea what harsh is."

"How about goodbye? Is that harsh enough fer you?"

"Sounds about right. Goodbye."

*　　*　　*

"Dear Father, who art in heaven- No, that's not what I am tryin' ta say."

Alan sat with his back at the base of the wall, knees bent up to his chest. He was wearing underwear and socks and covered in sweat.

"God, I have no idea what I'm doin'."

Tears clouded his bloodshot eyes.

"We haven't always been close. I'm sorry fer that, I really am. I'd probably like ta go back and remedy that, but that's topic for another discussion."

A Cross of St. Christopher was clenched in his palm.

"Lately, I've, I've been feelin' down. No, not just down, I've felt like shite, pardon my French. I'm not sure who I am, or what I am supposed ta be doin' with my life. I never 'magined I would grow up ta be tendin' bar in my thirties. I couldn't possibly imagine that I'd still be alone. Sometimes I feel like I am an alien on this planet. I'm not sure where that fits in biblically and all, but I trust that ya can understand what I mean. When I wake up there is almost a feeling of disappointment. That's probably not normal. It's not that I don't appreciate yer effort in creatin' all this down here, but ta be honest I'm a little let down. God, it seems like there are so many people out there who get just what they want and they are so unappreciative and meanwhile I get the short end of everyt'in' and I see that. Not ta be rude, but where is my fair lot? I don't need much, I'm not greedy or not'in'. No, all I'd like is a little bit of somet'in'. Somet'in', anyt'in', that shows me that ya love an' care fer me. I've read a lot, I've heard a lot, I know, well, I think I know, that ya care fer me, but I'd love ta see somet'in'."

* * *

Daibhead waited.

23.
cold and biting

Sorley sat perched at the window, peeking his beady eyes out, keeping watch behind the curtains.

"Yer a paranoid fat fuck, aren't ya?"

"Enough Fin, I don't need ta hear from ya right now."

"Well ya sure picked a helluva place not ta hear from me. Shall I leave my home?"

"Ya know what I mean, ya bastard. I don't wanna hear no talk 'f'her or that."

"'That'? Even I might call 'that' a bit cold. '*That*' is yer fat bastard child."

Sorley turned and shot an angry glance at his friend.

"Sorry."

"Ya should be."

"What ya gonna do?"

"Dunno."

"Run?"

"Maybe."

"Is this yer head start? I know yer a bit outta shape an' all but I t'ink considerin' yer walkin' distance from home she still might catch up."

"I dunno what I'm doin', okay? This is all kinda new ta me."

"Well, ta be honest, impregnating girlfriends isn't exactly a specialty mine, either. Perhaps we should call Niall."

"No, whatever ya do, don't call Dugan. Don't call anyone. I don't want anyone ta know I'm here, alright?"

"Sure, sure. Want me ta put the kettle on?"

"Alright, I'll have a spot of tea, t'anks."

"I was being sarcastic. I'm not that gooda host."

Fintan begrudgingly pulled an old iron kettle out of his cupboards and began to fill it with tap water.

"Why are ya so scared?"

"Jesus, we jus' met, hooked up, moved in, havin' a child, it's all goin' way too fast."

"I hear ya, we're barely in summer."

"I mean, I know I really like her, but that's obvious, everybody likes everybody at the beginning."

"I never liked ya."

"An' this jus' came outta nowhere, well not nowhere, cuz, ya know, we did it, that, and now it, *that*, is on the way."

"I'm surprised yer boys can even swim, y'ave issues at the wade pool."

"I don't even t'ink I'd make a good dad. That scares me. What if I'm shit? What if I'm responsible fer permanently ruinin' some poor child's life?"

"Two. Two children's lives. His an' yers."

"I never said I wanted ta be a da."

"I'm surprised she'd even let ya try."

"How am I goin' ta support a kid?"

"I'm amazed yer knees manage ta support yer weight."

The kettle was boiling and in his best imitation of being a good host Fintan found teacups with saucers and placed them on the table.

"Cheers. There's no way I'm ready fer this."

"The fact yer sittin' here is proof enough."

"What happens when Moira gets really big? What then? Will I be able ta help her out? Will I be runnin' off to store ta pick up pickles and ice cream?"

"I would've thought you'd be fully stocked in yer pantry."

"Fin, have I fucked up?"

"Yes, of course."

"What do I do?"

"I dunno, wanna call Dugan?"

*   *   *

Eoghan found Daibhead on the front step. He saw a young boy, not the man that his son was maturing into.

"Hello Daibh."

"Hi Da."

"Just putterin' 'round, are ya?"

"More'r less."

"Heard anyt'in' from yer girl?"

"No, not'in' yet."

"Ah, well don't let it get t'ya."

"Da?"

"Yes?"

"Is everyt'in' alright?"

Daibhead could sense something artificial and guarded in Eoghan's speech.

"I've gotta tell ya somet'in' 'bout yer Grampa."

"Yes?"

"It's bad."

"Oh."

"They say he hasn't got a lot left in his legs."

"How much longer?"

"Six weeks, two months max."

"How is he takin' it?"

"I t'ink he's doin' well. Ya should talk ta him."

"Yeh, I've been runnin' 'round so much I barely see him."

"He's jus' upstairs."

"Yeh."

*   *   *

"Hello Ms. Finnegan, what can I get ya?"

"Oh, jus' water, t'anks."

"Ya do realise this is a pub, yeh?"

"I know, Danny, I have other considerations at the moment."

Moira pointed downwards slyly. Doyle winked back in acknowledgment and fetched a glass of ice water.

"So am I right to assume that there is a little O'Mara on the way?"

"I hope he doesn't take too much after him."

"Oh, Sorley's a fine fella in a rough around the edges kind of way."

"That's what I thought."

"Not anymore?"

"He's ran away."

"Ran away?"

"Yeh. Two days ago. He was gone when I woke up."

"Y'aven't heard from him since?"

"No. That's why I'm here. I was hopin' you'd at least have seen him. Th'amount he frequents here I'd have t'ought he'd be in here hidin' in the corner."

"Sorry, Moira, I haven't seen yer man all week."

"Shit."

Danny looked at this weathered woman and saw someone who was methadone suicide pretty. The type of old broad whose leather exterior hid what a hundred thousand miles and fifteen years ago had once been a very attractive girl.

"Have ya seen his mates 'round?"

"Who, Niall Dugan or Fintan Larkin? Haven't seen either of them in at least three days. Quite odd, actually, Fintan is usually in here pissed drunk daily and Dugan is rarely far behind."

"Anyone else that would know of where he was?"

"He's somewhat close with the Farrell brothers. You can probably find Mícheál at his shop this time of day."

"Thanks, Danny, yer a gem."

"Spread the word."

"Always. Take care."

"I hope ya find him and talk some sense into his fat skull."

24.
some good they say

"Natalya, what are you doing looking out the window like some sort of voyeur?"

"Nothing, just looking out."

"You're lucky that the rowdy men over at the pub haven't caught wind of your sweet young body silhouetting through the drapery. That's how young girls like you end up pregnant and living off welfare."

"Looking out windows?"

"Yes, of course. It all starts innocently enough. First you're caught looking out windows by some surly ruffian. Next thing you know you're three children deep and living in a one-bedroom flat and the ruffian has floated off to some other small town to find some other young thing."

"How accurate are your predictions, mother?"

"Don't test me, Natalya."

"I'm not looking for any 'surly ruffians' or 'rowdy men', I am just looking to see if Daibhead is around."

"Daibhead Shannon?"

"Yes."

"He seems like a nice enough boy."

"I'm sure that's a glowing compliment from you."

"Well, I'm sure that he would be better than any number of the sort that frequent that pub."

"'He would be better' as what?"

"As a mate, of course. Why else would you be looking out the window?"

"Mother! I am not interested in Daibhead. We're just friends."

"Okay."

"Seriously."

"Well stay away from the window, then. I don't want you attracting the sex crazed now that they know you are single."

"I was single when you walked into the room."

"And I warned you then."

*   *   *

"Hi Marlene."

"Hello Nic. How are ya?"

"I'm real well, thanks. Yerself?"

"Good, good. What can I get ya?"

"Oh, uh, nothing. Actually, the reason I came in wasn't so much as to have a pint. I came in to talk to you."

"To me?"

"Yes, to you. I wanted to, how do I word this right? (I'm no good at this). Alright, let me just lay it all out there for you: I think you're absolutely gorgeous. Like, extremely beautiful. Just the way you are. Like today. The hair just the way it is. The clothes you wear. The whole damned thing about you."

"Wow."

"Now, I know we've never really, you know, talked much, that is, I've never really come in here and discussed more than the weather and that sort of small talk and I realise as I speak right now that I am just babbling on and failing at small talk, though I suppose this isn't a small talk situation, what with the whole saying you are absolutely gorgeous and all."

"Nicolás, I think the same thing."

"That's somewhat conceited."

"No, I mean about you. I think yer wonderful. Totally dashing."

"Oh! Well, thanks."

"I've thought it for a while."

"Would you like to have dinner with me sometime?"

"I'd love that."

"Okay. Dinner. Awesome. I need to leave. I have something to attend to, but thanks again for the compliment and I'll see you at dinner, sometime."

"Any day in particular?"

"Oh, right. Uh, how about tomorrow night?"

"I work tomorrow, but I am free the night after."

"That also works. Surprisingly enough, artists rarely have scheduled meetings to be at. Though, ironically, I must go now to just such an occasion."

"Oh, alright. We can arrange the details later."

"Excellent. See you later, Marla."

"Goodbye Nic."

*   *   *

"Grampa, you awake?"

"Come on in, Daibhead, I'm wide awake."

Lying in the bed was a man that Daibhead did not recognise from just weeks before and had surely passed in the house daily without notice.

"How are you feeling, Grampa?"

"Oh, jus' fine. Can't complain, no one will listen if I do."

"I'll listen."

"T'was a joke."

"Seriously, how are ya doin'? Da told me what the doctors say."

"He did, did he?"

"He did."

"Well, in that case, it's fair to say that I feel like shit, son."

Smiles briefly passed across both their faces.

*　　*　　*

Although the words
Once said, long ago
Now have drifted
Far, below the setting sun
They still linger
Here, here, here
In my mind
So that anywhere
I might go
They will come with me
To tease, to taunt
To toy, to haunt
To rip away at the flesh
Of whatever may remain
In me, the long forgotten man
Some spring's desire
Summer's discard
Autumn's disgust
Winter's despair

25.
on the road

"So what do I do?"

Danny's face pleaded an answer from the old man in the bed.

"Ya t'ink about what beauty is."

"Beauty? Paddy, I asked you about whether I should go on a trip
with Sara or not."

"Yes."

"So what does that have to do with me thinking about what
beauty is?"

"It has everyt'in' ta do with it."

"I'm more than a little confused."

"Tha's why yer askin' a dying man fer advice."

"Are you taking the piss?"

"No. Even though I still have a little vinegar in me, the last t'ing
I'd do is steer ya wrong. T'ink about beauty."

"Beauty."

"Beauty fer me, a long time ago, meant sittin' on my old back
porch, sippin' whiskey, watchin' the sunset."

"What does it mean now?"

"Lyin' here, seein' Eoghan, Daibhead an' yerself come ta me as
men, askin' mature questions, that's beautiful. I've always
thought'f'ya as family, Danny. You'll always be another
son ta me."

"Thank you, that means a lot. I'm going to go take care of
something. I'll talk to you later."

"I'll be right here."

*   *   *

"Ya see, Sorley, this is where life is."

Sorley O'Mara looked at the grinning snarl of Niall Dugan and then over at his friend Fintan Larkin who looked equally amused.

"Welcome back ta the city."

*　　*　　*

Moira was welcomed into the butcher's shop with the sound of a small bell. The elder Farrell brother was behind the counter, placing out strips of lamb, lined in a row, each one looking more delicious than the last.

"Those look good."

"Ah, hi, Moira. Can I wrap one up for ya? Or two, I s'pose ol' Sorley will want one as well."

"Sorry, no, none taday. I came t'ask ya 'bout'm, actually."

"Sure, what about him?"

"Have ya seen'm?"

"No, I haven't, should I have?"

"Nevermind."

"Sorry?"

"He's run off. I thought maybe ya'd know where'e is."

"I reckon he'd be with Fin or Niall, or worse yet, both."

"Tha's jus' it, I've gone 'round ta their places an' they're not 'round. They're not at the pub, neither."

"How long has he been off?"

"Couple days, now."

"And ya haven't heard from him?"

"No."

"That's odd, I thought you'd been getting on rather well lately."

174

"We had. Well, it is, we were 'til I told him I was expectin'."

Mícheál looked at her with a more interested face.

"And that's when he left?"

"Not right away, but sometime early in the mornin', 'fore I
    woke. He'd skipped out, without a sound."

"Bastard."

"Yeah, but I love'm."

*　　*　　*

I've been hanging on so long
Sitting around
Waiting for you to call
And all I know now
Is that was the wrong way to go

I've been hanging on so long
Sitting around
Hating on myself
And all I've discovered
Is that was the wrong way to go

Love me
I'm not begging you
I'm letting you know
You ought to love me
If you love yourself
And you see what's right

*　　*　　*

"Saraid, let me start by saying, I am so sorry."

"What for?"

"I know that I've been a total cementhead with you. I know that
    you almost left for good."

"And?"

"And, and, and I don't want you to leave town without me. I'm not saying I want to go today. But, yes, yes, I will go with you. To wherever. We just need to sort a few things out. But, yes, I love you."

"I love you too, Danny. That's what's so hard."

"I'm sorry for that. I've been guarded."

"That's an understatement, if I've ever heard one. You're so 'guarded' that I don't know where we're at. One day I think you want to spend the rest of your life with me. Other days I have no clue. Tell me what day it is."

"Today is unequivocally a day where I want nothing more than to be with you."

"And tomorrow?"

"Tomorrow will be the same."

"And the day after?"

"The same."

"What happens when the winds change or the tides go in and out?"

"The same. I want to be with you forever."

"How can you say that?"

"Because I am done looking for easy answers. I'm tired of drifting. I've let inertia pull me down so long that I know that I have to break out and you're the only person I know that can help."

"But can I make you happy?"

"Of course. I'm not an unhappy person. I'm unfulfilled."

"What would fulfill you, Daniél Doyle?"

"A challenge."

"A challenge?"

"Yes, and you're the biggest one I know."

      *   *   *

"Go ahead, Sorley, just a blip."

26.
the ties that bind

"She's amazing."

"The waitress?"

"Yes. Marla Cullen."

"What's so amazing about her?"

"I think she's gorgeous."

"She's alright. She's no Saraid Doran."

"What's that got to do with it?"

"Well, if you're gonna make a play, why not shoot for the stars?"

"But I don't really like Sara."

"She's the best looking girl in town, what's not to like?"

"I'm trying to tell you about Marla."

"And I'm trying to tell you that she ain't Sara Doran."

"Well, what the hell does that have to do with it anyway?"

"I just think that Sara makes a far better match. She's well suited
for anything."

"But I like Marla Cullen."

"The waitress?"

"Yes. My God, we've gone over this."

"Well, what's so special about her?"

"I already told you, I think she's gorgeous."

"And I already told you, she's no Saraid Doran."

"Will you let it go?"

"No, tell me a different reason why you like Marla. Her being
attractive isn't enough. Like I said, there's an easy example
of someone who's more attractive. That's not a reason to
like someone, being the second most attractive girl you see
at the pub."

"Her personality."

"What about it?"

"I think Marla has a great personality."

"So does Paddy. You want to date him?"

"Yer being ridiculous."

"No, Nic, you are being ridiculous. I can't believe that you see anything worthwhile in Marla Cullen."

"Yer an ass. I didn't come here to argue with you. I wanted to tell you that I'm going to be seeing Marla and I thought as my brother you'd cheer me on. Thanks a lot."

*   *   *

If I just sit here
A little longer
Maybe you'll show
If I just sit here
A little longer
Maybe you'll show

Or maybe not
My head is spinning
Around and around

If I just sit here
Be a bit stronger
Maybe you'll know
If I just sit here
Be a bit stronger
Maybe you'll know

Or maybe not
My head is spinning
Around and around
Again

*   *   *

Alan sat at the window, staring vacantly outward.

*   *   *

"This distance, the waiting, time, space - it's all killing me."

Daibhead realised his choice of words immediately and looked at his grandfather with a look of desperate humility.

"Sorry."

"Don't be. Jus' because someone in reality may be in a far more serious state than you doesn't take away from what ya feel an' experience. If ya feel like it is killing you - that nagging, clawing, tearing feeling inside - well, then, that is what ya feel. Not'in' can dispute that."

"Really?"

"Yes, it's forgivable. Like being really hungry an' claimin' yer starvin'. Hyperbole, yes. But it's what ya feel at the time."

"I guess I've never thought about it that way."

"Don't. The last t'ing I want ya ta do is ta t'ink yer way outta feelin'. There are far too many people in the world that no longer feel the slightest shift in emotion an' are often struck down when the tempests hit because they could not anticipate the fatal blow's arrival."

The younger Shannon put his hand on the elder's shoulder.

"I miss her."

"I know."

"I'm goin' ta miss you."

"I know."

"It's not fair. Everyt'in' is slippin' outta my hands. What am I left with?"

Pádraig closed his eyes for a moment and let the thought linger in his head before he responded.

"Yer left with yer hands."

"My hands?"

"Yes, those hands. What ya see as empty are really hands of potential. They will make somet'in' outta all this. You will make somet'in', Daibhead."

"What?"

"I don't know. Despite all the sage advice oozing outta my pores at this late stage I don't know. That's somet'in' fer you."

"Where do I look?"

"Daibhead, please. Look in the mirror."

*   *   *

"What are you looking at?"

Sara startled him with her stealth approach.

"Jus' lookin'."

"Nothing in particular?"

"No."

"Can I have a word?"

"Okay."

"Alan, I want to let you know that I'm in love with Daniél."

"I know that."

"He's in love with me."

"I know that, too."

"Alan, we're going to leave town."

"Where to?"

"Don't know yet."

"Why are ya tellin' me this?"

"I just, you know, want you to hear it from me."

"I don't love you Saraid."

"Don't say it to make me feel better. I just don't want you to be hurt. We're all still worried about you."

"'Worried'? 'Worried' like when everyone was laughin' at my expense?"

"They didn't know."

"How could they not know? I've spent the better part'f my life bein' miserable."

"I guess that's how it goes unnoticed."

27.
crying never felt so good

"Oh, Sorley, how could ya leave me like this?"

Moira petitioned the empty chair where her lover had so often sat. She listened for the slightest of sounds to escape. Unsurprisingly, it gave back little comfort to the lonely woman. What more could she beg of the inanimate objects in her home? She had pleaded for some semblance of sanity and repose. Sorley, Sorley, Sorley, she missed him so. What ached the most was her expectant heart, oft-searching for some consolation of her worth. Why go, why? What had she done to provoke and awake the slumbering beast inside O'Mara? He had come so far in their time together that she had seen a nascent man rise up and meet what life asks of men to be. He had been strong. He had held her in his arms and protected her from the attacks of the world.

"Who's ta hold me now?"

Moira's arms barely traversed her body without beginning to tremble.

* * *

Curled in the doorway, a forgotten soul, far, far from home, I sat. Nestled in my cloak, Teague Grady, the traveling troubadour. I rubbed my hands together for warmth on that cold, summer's night. My tussled hair, as you see me now, it flowed from the top of my head seamlessly into my beard. The streetlights lit up my face when I turned their direction and I could sometimes see my breath, even though it was July. It was on that night, that it all began to click in my head. I began mumbling to myself a tale, from some past life, of a man who lost everything because of his pride. Slowly, my prose grew and grew, until it found a beat and I began to sing:

Come, come back
I know things will be different
This time, for sure
I've got my head on straight
I've learned a few things
And I will anticipate

You've got to anticipate the dark
When you see the sunset
Fall over your head

You've got to anticipate the rain
Before you get wet
Clouds over your head

I'm trying to find my feet
I'm trying to find my feet
I'm trying to find my feet

Oh Molly, have you seen them?

*   *   *

Eoghan re-read the newspaper clipping. This woman, this extremely young woman, had been his mother. He had known nothing of her. She was just a name, an age and a picture of a wreck on the side of the road. She had left him to be raised alone by his father. *What a mother.* She had been so young. Younger than most of his barstaff. That was no excuse. She had been selfish.

"She had tried to kill me."

His head felt like it had been kicked-in a hundred times. His entire life he had longed to know of her. Had she loved him? She had left his life before he knew she existed. Like a boy who loses his innocence too soon, Eoghan wanted his father to take back everything he had said about Maeve Hogan. *Maeve Hogan*. Not his mother. She was not his mother. She was Maeve Hogan, 24, of Donegal town, deceased January 17th, 1970 in an automobile accident.

Those were the only facts he knew. The rest of his life and his connection to her were blurred in the memories of a dying man.

"Take it all back, Pádraig. I'd wish I'd never heard it."

But he was alone. Alone, Eoghan Shannon and the truth. It couldn't be taken back for all his wishes; it stared back at him from the wreckage. Like that boy, once realising his innocence can never return, Eoghan collapsed. The tears, like glacial waterfalls, fell coolly on his smolten cheeks. Maybe tomorrow it will return, he hoped against all knowledge, maybe tomorrow.

28.
a proper date

Saraid had never felt so right in so long. Lying on the blanket next to her was the man she loved. Danny was turned on his side, easily gazing into the eyes of the most beautiful woman he would ever see.

"Well, this is shit then, I guess we're through."

He spritefully smiled at her bemused face.

"Never thought it would last."

Sara Doran prayed that it would go on forever. In front of her she saw a future that held her like only the formidable Mr. Doyle could. There would be no other, just like there had been none before nor since their lives past.

"Do you love me?"

"Yes. Most certainly."

"Most certainly?"

"With the most certainty, I do. I love you more than I believe that gravity keeps me planted to this earth."

"I love you, too."

"You do?"

"Infinitely."

"Infinitely?"

"I love you beyond the depths of the unknown universe."

"And, what of my depths?"

"I love you for the man you hide inside you. And, I love you for the boyish charm you call a gatekeeper."

"Boyish charm?"

"The most."

"That's it: I'm going home."

"Did I forget to kick the back of your chair?"

"And pull my hair also."

"Much forgiveness, I beg of you."

Sara pounced on her willing victim.

"Please, Madam, if only you'd let me go. I have a choir meeting
to be at."

"Yes, a shame you'll miss it. Your voice could use some work."

"I've been having private lessons. Have you not noticed?"

"I have. You ought to ask for your money back."

"I would, though I received them in exchange for doing some
household cleaning."

"Perhaps you could mess up your tutor's home again."

"I couldn't, I can't help but worry about what the choir master
would say."

"He doesn't need to know."

"It was his house."

"Shame."

Daniél acquiesced to her presence atop him and let out a relaxive
sigh.

"Where do you want to go on our adventure?"

"Anywhere. But you have to take me."

"That shouldn't be hard. I think I'd like to go somewhere by
accident. Just show up and ask for a ticket for the next
train, wherever it goes."

"They all go to Dublin from here."

"Then to Dublin we shall go."

"Hardly an adventure. I go in once a week. We need to leave Ireland for a while."

"The first train that leaves I'll go."

"Clever boy. Let's fly to London and train from there. Paris, Bruges, wherever."

"Je ne parle pas beaucoup du français."

"Pas grave, mon amour. Tu m'as, et mon amour est suffisimment."

"Je t'aime. Pour maintenant et toujours. Je veux tu partir jamais."

"Je ne vais pas n'importe où sans tu."

Daniél lifted his head enough to kiss the top of her head resting on his chest.

* * *

"It's funny we've never really talked much before."

"It is. I don't know why that is. It's a small enough town and there are so few decent people that I am amazed we've never been drawn together before."

"Is it our age difference, perhaps?"

"Perhaps. You're what nineteen, twenty?"

"Yes. Twenty this fall."

"So when I was your age you were far too young to be noticed."

"And you were too cool ta notice."

Nic watched Marla's body language and saw an expressive soul reaching for a moment to explode and reveal herself. He took a chance and grabbed her hand as they walked along the river.

"T'anks, it was beginnin' ta get a little cold."

"I'm sorry if I came off really lame, it's been a long time."

"It's okay, Nic, it's been never fer me."

His heart began to beat with a tad more oomph as he gained confidence. Beside him tonight was the loveliest lady he knew and she was a blank canvas.

"Favourite singer?"

"Depends on my mood."

"Tonight?"

"Katie Melua. She sings with such a smooth effortlessness. It's natural, comforting an' jus' feels right."

"I like that."

"I suppose it's my turn t'ask y'a question. If ya could go anywhere fer jus' one day, anywhere in the whole world, where would ya go?"

"Only one day, well I'd have to say London. I mean by the time I get to the airport, go through security and so on, I've got maybe half the day left. Might as well take the short hop over, spend an hour at the Nat and fly back."

"I said anywhere."

"With like a teleport machine?"

"Yes."

"Can I travel through time?"

"No. This only travels through space, not time."

"So then I could go anywhere in the universe."

"No, this is a very limited teleport machine that has a governor that restricts trips t'within our atmosphere."

"Everest."

"Really?"

"I would bring my easel and paint the scenery. Me, alone at the peak, surrounded by a kind of majestic beauty that only the hungriest of men have seen."

"And all without workin' up a sweat."

"Exactly. You?"

"Is there any room on that mountain for me?"

29.
what aches?

"How am I supposed to be okay with this?"

Natasha looked across at the elder woman and felt nothing but empathy, as if her own husband had himself ran off.

"You're not. Tressa, be strong. Strong in who you are. But, not so strong as to bottle up emotion. It's okay to cry. Don't let it define you, though. That's when Liam wins."

"Thank you, I needed a friend and yer a very generous one."

"I don't get why he leaves. You have a beautiful home. Family. Your meals are delicious. He's a very lucky man. Sergei should ask for so much."

"Sergei is a lucky man. He has you. You must keep him grounded. Liam was never like that. In his own world, his letters, his boxes. Ideas, ideas, ideas. All that ever materialised were ideas. I didn't keep him grounded, I chained him to a tether and let his mind float away until one day the tether snapped."

"But a man should know he cannot fly. Like Icarus and Atticus."

"Liam was exactly that, he flew up, up, up, until he collided with the sun and came back to earth in flames on melting wax wings."

"You were the wings."

"Yes, I was. I encouraged him. I pushed him ta write. He was always a great poet. I wanted him ta finish somet'in'."

"Did he?"

"No. He said he was done. I had drained him. His job had drained him. Ireland had drained him."

"So you were the sun too."

"When it comes ta Liam Bradigan I was the sun, the moon, the wax wings an' the ocean he hit when he flew too high."

"And now?"

"Now I am just Tressa. A name on his mailing list, somewhere
high enough t'warrant a letter but low enough ta justify
not sendin' an invitation his wedding."

*   *   *

Daibhead stirred up all his anticipatory anger and delved head
first in. Hell felt no fury like the paper felt his pen. He had tried
so hard to contain his emotions, but to no avail. There were
breaking points for all men and Daibhead had breached his
threshold.

Dear Ánna,

*What do you want from me? Is it silence? Something that I can't bear
to give you, but is given to me infinitely? What? I love you like no boy
ought to, but as every man should. I shoulder a burden that is crippling
me. I sit and I wait and I listen for the hope remains in me that one day
the phone might ring and your voice will crackle on the other side. How
long will I have to wait? It seems like forever. That's too long. I said I'd
love you forever. I meant it. I really did. But I'm only now realising
how long forever really is. It's almost been three months since I saw
you leave. Three months. And I've heard so little from you. Some
assurance would make all the difference. To wake and see something
from you awaiting me. To wake and read words of comfort. God, it is
killing me.*

*I'm not bitter, really. I respect what you're doing and why you want to
do it. It's hard not to. You've got a heart that is so rare and those
children are probably all in love with you. But what about me? I'm
probably too selfish for my own good. I'd love to have you beside me
right now. To comfort me. To tell me things will be okay. My
grandfather is dying. Tell me I'll be okay. Please.*

He shoved the letter in an envelope and stuffed it under his
pillow.

*   *   *

Why you always leading me astray?
Now you're here and happy
Tomorrow's some other day
Why you always leading me astray?

Why you always leading me astray?
Now you're good and certain
But tomorrow you won't pray
Why you always leading me astray?

Why you always leading me astray?
Now you tell me all your feelings
Tomorrow you keep them at bay
Why you always leading me astray?

Why you always leading me astray?
Now you love no other
But tomorrow you can't say
Why you always leading me astray?

Why you always leading me astray?
Now we lie together
Tomorrow, the gutter, I'll lay
Why you always leading me astray?

*   *   *

Mícheál looked at the blueprints and smiled. Maybe, someday soon, they might be more than that.

30.
in the heat of summer

"Can I trust ya ta keep a secret?"

Alan's timid questioning put Mícheál in an awkward place.

"Sure, I mean, yes. Yes, you can trust me."

"I t'ink there's somet'in' wrong with me."

"Wrong with you?"

"Yes. I'm, how do I say this, I'm gay."

Mícheál looked at his friend and saw a man who had finally spoken the most honest words of his life.

"That's great. Honestly, there's nothing wrong with you."

"It just feels so wrong."

"Does it?"

"Well, not the feelin', admittin' ta myself is fine, but more just knowin' that other people would know that about me."

"Ya can't worry about what other people think or say. There's a lot of eejits out there and if you let them dictate how you live then yer an even bigger eejit."

"It took me a long time t'admit it. But it worries me."

"Like I said, don't worry about what other people will say."

"But what about God?"

"I'm not religious, Alan, but what I'd assume, from what I've heard about yer God, He's going to love you for being you. I've my doubts about His existence, but, if He can't love what He made then He's a hypocritical creator and no God for me."

"T'anks."

*   *   *

"That's it, boys, break it up!"

Sorley saw the Gardaí and knew they were fucked. How did this escalate so quickly? Fintan and Niall had proven once again that they didn't know the proper point when to shut their yaps and let something go. What would Moira say now? *Moira.* How could he have ran away from her to join these fools? Nothing but trouble, always. They said they had his back and they meant it, but only after they'd dragged him into a brawl and he needed them to help fend off the angry mob. Some friends.

"Let's go. You'll be spendin' the night at the station."

Sorley's only consolation was that neither Dugan nor Larkin put up any resistance and kept their mouths shut for once.

*   *   *

Natalya woke to the rapping at her window. Some small pebbles had been thrown from the ground below. Rising out of bed to look out the window she saw Daibhead standing there.

"What is he doing?"

She opened the window and leaned out to project her whisper.

"Daibhead! What are you doing, you'll wake everyone up."
"I'm sorry. I tried ta be as quiet as possible. Get dressed and come out with me."

His face was flush red and his eyes were the size of saucers, lit up under the moonlight.

"I hate you. I'll be down in five."

31.
a masterpiece

Eoghan found himself in the basement sorting through old cardboard boxes that hadn't been open in twenty years. Everything had an aura around it that it belonged to someone else, though they all contained remnants of his childhood. Dusty memories lingered. One box was labeled 'toys' in Paddy's distinctive scrawl. Eoghan pulled it down and placed it on the ground in front of him, peeling back the fraying cardboard and the tape that barely held any stick.

How long it had been for Eoghan to even think of his childhood. It had been forever ago. Before Daibhead, before Grace, how much of the shoreline had eroded since then?

Pokey sat there in that box staring back up at Eoghan with his one remaining button eye. Ah, Pokey, his bear. The one that his father made himself. Sewn together scraps of fabric with button eyes and he called it love. It was. It was magic. How many boys could say that their father could sew a bear? How many boys could say their father could even sew? Here, years later he saw the man that his dad had been. Pádraig was everything to him, alpha and omega, the man who could catch a fish and then cook it, too. He embodied everything that Eoghan had tried to live up to. A man who was firm when it mattered, but knew when to show compassion. A man who held his beliefs and let nothing compromise them, save love. Eoghan respected Pádraig for raising him on his own and when Grace passed he saw for himself how difficult it actually is.

Eoghan could only hope that he had passed on the same values to his son. Daibhead was still a little rough around the edges but had shown at times that he was a man-in-waiting. Respectful and respected.

Though he probably had no idea where he wanted to go in life, Eoghan was certain that Daibhead was definite in how he wanted to get there. To the Shannon family, the ends never justified the means. Actions defined them. Better to be inactive than to dishonour yourself. Pádraig had taught him at a young age that to build a reputation takes a lifetime, to destroy it but a second.

* * *

"That was some bad craic last night."

"D'ya remember when ya grabbed that fella by the neck and threw him through the window?"

"I do. He had no idea."

Sorley couldn't believe what he was hearing. Fifteen minutes out of the station and they were already reminiscing.

"We're lucky we're not being charged."

Niall scowled at Sorley. Fintan was less harsh.

"I hear ya, Sorley. Sorry."

"That? That was not'in', O'Mara. Remember that one time when you and I got caught fer lightin' t'ings on fire? We were far more likely ta be charged then."

"That was a long time ago. I'm not inta causin' shit nomore."

"Ya sure didn't act that way last night."

"It's a little difficult t'excuse myself from a brawl when I've got two jackeens throwing punches at me."

Sorley was at the point where he was done with Dugan, Larkin, and Dublin.

"I t'ink it's time I go back ta Moira."

* * *

"Top of your class?"

"Top of my class."

"Everyone?"

"Everyone."

"Maksim, I am very proud of you."

"Thank you."

"We must go out tonight for dinner to celebrate."

"Really?"

"Yes, of course. You've put your energy into something and
shown what you are capable of. I'm honestly very proud of
you, son."

Sergei's pride was bursting out of his pores. He couldn't believe
that he was the father of such a promising young scholar. All of
his struggles to support his family and bring them to Ireland had
begun to show some fruition. In Maks' success he realised why
Pádraig had warned him of being too harsh. This boy was
certainly capable of something beyond the grocery.

*   *   *

Marla, blindfolded, left hand being guided by Nic's, walked
timidly into the room.

"Can I take off the blindfold?"

"Not just yet."

"Okay."

Nicolás left her standing there and went to the covered easel ten
feet in front of them. He carefully removed the bedsheet that was
slung over. He looked at his creation, one last selfish, secret look,
before he was to reveal its existence.

"Okay, you can take it off."

She slowly removed the erstwhile bandana and saw.

"Wow."

Looking across at her was herself. It wasn't a mirrored image, the external superficialities that anyone could see, no; it wasn't that. Staring her in the face was a portrait of her heart: frail, bruised, and naked. The fresco's seeped style spoke to her. She had long tried to hide her wounds, but like the fresh layer of cream skin over the purple backdrop, they were visible to the right eyes. Nicolás' eyes.

"That's me, isn't it?"

"It is."

"How?"

"I don't know. I painted that a while ago. Before."

"But, it's so-"

"You."

"It is."

Marlene Cullen, the person, wept at the sight of Marlene Cullen, the portrait. She was flawed, ugly, broken and near perfect.

"I love it."

32.
the big plan

"Alright, Sorley, here's the deal: ya walk in that door, say 'hello', an' act as'f not'in' is the matter."

"That, Niall, is the single worst idea I've ever heard."

"Jus' tryin' ta help."

"I'm beginnin' t'ink that yer help ain't so helpful."

"Alright, alright. I'll try a bit harder."

"T'anks, much appreciated."

"I've got a few t'oughts, myself."

Sorley looked at Fintan and saw the first honest look he's seen from his best friend in what felt like years.

"Go 'head."

"Ya can't jus' walk back an' pretend like not'in' happened. I'm takin' a wild guess that Moira is prolly pretty pissed at ya."

"Yeh."

"You've gotta come back - *different* - than when ya left."

"How so?"

"Why'd ya run away in the first place?"

"I was scared."

"Of what?"

"Of a lotta things. I was scared'f being a father. Of being responsible for somet'in' small, like that. I didn't want ta be a fuck-up, or not'in'. I didn't want ta mess up the kid's life, Moira's, an' prolly, most'f all, my own. I've already sucked at that."

Even Niall Dugan was beginning to see that this was important. The three of them had spent their lives amounting to very little, at no fault but their own.

"Sorley, I wanna apologise, what fer the trouble I've gotcha in."

"T'anks, but it's as much my fault. Moira warned me 'bout hangin' 'round ya fellas, fearin' you was bad influences, but I'm as much ta blame. I'm thirty years old an' I walked inta this. Nobody dragged me."

Thoughts were starting to rumble around in the sobering mind of Fin Larkin.

"You have ta tell her all this."

"What?"

"Yer fears. Yer thoughts. All'f it."

"What good'll that do now? I've ran away from the best t'ing that happened ta me. Who runs from that? What was I t'inkin'?"

"Ya weren't, Sor, ya weren't. But, if there's any chance gettin' her back, ya best be goin' now. Y'ave got ta show her that ya realise what's best fer ya, an' that's her."

*   *   *

"It was a wilder time, back then."

"Yeh."

"Ya can't understand it, if ya weren't there, it was hectic, *crazy*, even. Political turmoil, you've seen that, but this was a time when that stuff extended beyond Ulster. It boiled down south, too. When yer mother left for Donegal I'd worried for her safety, the bombings, maybe. Crossing Derry. That, that, that sort of thing. I'd never expected she'd do herself in by a traffic collision. Never."

Eoghan sat beside his father, just trying to soak up anything and everything the old man would give.

"It's strange, Eoghan; I was much older than Maeve and I had thought that she would naturally outlive me. Here I am, an elderly man, one who's lived a very full life, been blessed many times over, an' I'll never know whether she felt any'f that in her short time on this earth."

"It's hard to say with those t'ings, Da. When Grace passed, there was, I guess, at the very least a sense that she knew she was loved. We had many restless nights at the hospital, sitting, remembering. I don't know whether my mother had any'f those moments, but perhaps, I don't t'ink it would be unreasonable t'assume, she may have had one. She may have known."

"Ah, Eoghan, yer getting ta be too much like yer old man, waxin' on."

"Has ta come from somewhere."

"Agreed. It also has ta go somewhere, when the time comes. If it won't make ya uncomfortable, I'd like to discuss my burial."

"It's going ta be uncomfortable, but we should."

"I wanna be buried in my village. Next ta my parents. I never got 'long well with Lochlan, but we can still be neighbours."

*　　*　　*

"We should get an unlimited rail pass."

"I like that. Then we don't need to worry about planning too far ahead."

Sara saw Danny with a spark in his eyes as he said it. He was always planning too far ahead. He just rarely shared those thoughts with anyone. She watched him pour over the maps and travel books and it became clear that he had a general idea where he wanted to go.

"So, where to first?"

"Paris."

"So definitive, Daniél Doyle."

"Well, Saraid, I've heard that it is among the most romantic places on this planet, and I figure we might as well do that first, in case the trip goes horribly wrong."

"Yeah, nothing like traveling for months and becoming embittered and then having to finish with the romance."

"Ha, could you imagine all the lovey-doveys frolicking along Champs-Élysées while we sit awkwardly at a café?"

"'Do you want to go up the Eiffel Tower, Danny?' 'Feck off, Sara.'"

They laughed a careless laughter that would have been unthinkable just weeks prior.

"I love you Sara, and I want to begin this trip affirming that."

"Can we go shopping?"

She grinned mischievously, then acquiesced to his sentiment with a warm smile.

"Danny, have I ever told you how much I enjoy just looking at you?"

"Go on."

"When I enter a room and you are in it, I just get butterflies, not just in my stomach, but throughout my body. Goosebumps, really. There is something mystical about you, something that has great power, you can flash a small smile and it warms the whole room up."

"I feel the same way about you. It's funny you say that I have some sort of power, but I honestly feel nothing but vulnerability around you. You have all the power in the world."

"Danny, I don't feel like I have any power at all. I just know that when I come hug you and bury myself in your chest, there is nothing outside that can harm me. I feel completely safe."

She inched closer and closer to him, butterflies everywhere, until his arms enveloped her.

33.
my conscience is one thing i can't beat down

There is a great burden on all of us, as we slink slowly towards the end. We head out filled with memories of past conquests and failures, alike, lining the brain without order or reason. The things that grab our attention at odd moments sometimes serve a greater purpose, and at other times, just are, without explanation. We tell ourselves the great lie, that everything happens for a reason, when, surely, that cannot be. Some things, may, indeed, happen to fulfill some requisite steps on our paths, and others may just happen. We sit here, tonight, three sheets to the wind, as I unwind the tale of my time in some village, all without me knowing right now whether this meeting was serendipitous, that it was guided by fate or fortune, that it means something. Or, is this just the rambling of a drunken traveler on a random night, fueled by spirit? I don't know now, and it may take some time, and perhaps, then, far from now, I'll be able to reflect on this passing evening as part of a bigger picture for what my life has become. Or not.

*   *   *

"Marla, can you keep a secret?"

Marla Cullen looked at the girl across from her, not that much younger than herself, looking back expectantly, with eyes filled with admiration.

"Sure, I s'pose that I can, Natalya, but I dunno 'f'I'm really th'one y'ought ta be tellin'."

"I thought it would be easier to talk with you because you are young enough to understand, but not one of my close friends, who are likely to keep the secret for two days and then lead to gossip."

"Oh."

"So, can I trust you?"

Natalya was stepping out onto a ledge that bounded an abyss.

"You can."

"About a week ago, a guy came by my house at night."

The last thing Marla wanted to hear was the intimate relations of near strangers.

"Uh, Nat, perhaps we shouldn't be havin' this talk."

"No. No, no. It's not what you think. Nothing like that. He came by and then we left, heading down towards the river to talk."

"Oh."

"It's kinda complicated. He has a girlfriend already, but they are, well, to put it simply, they are going through a tough patch, and he's developed feelings for me."

"Nat, don't bother 'f'he has a girlfriend."

"I know you are saying that. And, for sure, a part of me is saying get out right now. Go far from this guy, because the last thing I want to do is interfere when he is already involved. I should let that go on its own. I don't need to push or pull, or any of that, right?"

"Right."

"But, the thing is, it doesn't look promising, and if it is going to end, and he's already said that he expects it to end sometime, why shouldn't I step up, and say, 'yes', why shouldn't I make myself available to him?"

"As long as he still has a girlfriend, Nat, yer jus' leavin' yerself open ta hurt."

"But he said they might break up."

"Might. But ya dunno when."

"He said it sounds like soon, and I don't wanna lose him. He is really wonderful."

"He may be, but he's unavailable, 'f'y'ave any respect fer his current situation."

"But it's on its last legs. Why can't I help push him along by sharing my feelings for him?"

"What would ya do 'f'ya were th'other gal?"

Natalya had already had that thought, and no amount of bargaining was going to solve how it made her feel.

"It's not fair. He is wonderful. I don't think she knows that. I do, and I think we'd be terrific together."

"Ya may be, but tha's not the case, an' it's not yer place ta change it. Right now, yer best to stay on the outside lookin' in. Yer job is ta be a great friend, when he needs one, an' that is it."

"What if it is too hard to see him everyday? What if it is too hard to hear the words he says about her? Knowing that, no matter what, he isn't mine?"

"Then y'ave t'walk away."

*   *   *

She said it's all just bad timing with us
Bad timing in my head, she said
She doesn't think she can
Afford to fall in love
Afford to fall in love, today

Maybe
Maybe tomorrow
We might fit it in
But it's busy then

I don't profess to know the answers
I don't know, she said
I don't know when I'll ever be ready
Ready to fall in love

Maybe
Maybe someday
We might fit it in
But, until then

We are just victims

*   *   *

Moira listened as the words came out of Sorley, slow, deliberative, almost eloquent; he spoke from a place that hadn't existed before he met her. He told her everything. His fears were now theirs. And then he ended, with the most moving words she would ever hear, and he would ever say.

"I've got no solution fer ya, jus' my own setta problems, and new problems we'll create. I'm not promisin' t'whisk y'off yer feet an' take y'away t'a place where problems don't exist. I can't do that. Problems will come an' go, an' some will just stick around an' linger, but my God, I love ya. Is that enough?"

34.
something's not right

Sergei Abramov stared at the front page of the *Independent* in disbelief. On the eve of the Olympics, a sporting event meant to embody world peace, his countrymen had begun an armed conflict in their backyard against some long-gone former republic over marginal territory neither had any real control over. The summer's heat was finally beginning to be felt in those dog days and Sergei couldn't wait for fall showers to wash this all away.

*   *   *

Something, a little understated
It slips through the mind
Something, a little underrated
I just want mine
To fill the void and my time
Oh, I just want to sing

Sing, a lovely song, a lovely song, a lovely song
Away, a lovely song, a lovely song

The girl at the corner
She works three shifts in a day
Struggling to pay the bills
She still believes, still believes
That something waits out there for her
Won't you take her away, and,

Sing, a lovely song, a lovely song, a lovely song
Away, a lovely song, a lovely song

The boy in the shop
Selling used parts of his heart
And his heart will go on
But, when, and where, and why, and how?
Don't know the answer right now
Who's going to take him away, and

Sing, a lovely song, a lovely song, a lovely song
Away, a lovely song, a lovely song

And, I'm afraid of what's out there
And, I'm afraid of what I'll find
Maybe disappointment
Maybe a big let down
Maybe, maybe, maybe, maybe, maybe

Maybe I'll just sing a lovely song

So, sing a lovely song to him
And, sing a lovely song to her
A lovely song, a lovely song
Say you'll take them away
A lovely song, a lovely song

*   *   *

Disappointment builds up rather quickly, and silence, though intended to be neutral in nature, leads to disappointment's victory. If only a single affirming word could seep out of the void and find itself in Daibhead Shannon's head. Why did Ánna leave him nothing satisfactory? A single word is all it would take.

*   *   *

"Y'alright, then Alan?"

Doyle's voice barely reached Alan's ears. He was too distant.

Too far from where Alan Brennan was.

"Hmm? What's that?"

"Y'alright?"

"I am. Yes. T'anks."

He wasn't. Of course not. How many weeks had passed since he had walked up that bridge? Eight, maybe nine? A darkness surrounded Alan wherever he went, and yet he felt no one else seemed to notice. How was it possible? How was it possible to feel so miserable and feel so alone? Why was he the only one suffering?

*   *   *

"Ya goddamn Russians. Why didya have ta go an' put a damper on a day like taday? I was wantin' watch th'opening ceremonies without no trouble an' ya had ta go an' ruin it, ya bastards."

"Fin, I've lived in this town for years. You know that I had nothin' to do with what's going on over there."

Fintan's bloodshot eyes stared contemptuously at Maksim. What a bastard, he thought. How dare he plead ignorance? It was those Russians that had started so many conflicts before.

"Ya can say that you've lived here, but we both know which one of us is Irish."

"My passport says I am Irish, Fintan. That's all that matters."

"Yer bloody passports. All ya care 'bout is passports. Fuckin' EU. Why don't ya go back to Dublin and live with yer Polish friends. This is bullshit. This is my town."

Enraged, Fin Larkin rose from the barstool and stormed to the door. He opened it up and turned to the room.

"Outside this door, ya bastards, is a street that my great-grandfather built. He tore up the old cobblestone with his own hands. The last t'ing he'd want ta see is this unappreciative Russian bastard making money sellin' fags an' crisps ta you lot. I'm not goin' ta spend one more euro supportin' the fuckin' Russians."

35.
i promise

When you know, you just know. It could be something as simple as a first formal introduction at a casual setting, like a wine and cheese gathering, an accidental intervention on the part of destiny that you wind up next to that someone. There are just too many ways that can lead those two people together, but once they are there, together, finally, after perhaps an entire life searching for each other, well, as you know, it can be electric. Nic knew he loved Marla before he knew it was Marla that he loved.

"Where are we?"

Marlene Cullen walked gingerly up the side of the hill, careful to avoid stepping in one of the many mud pockets that coated the green countryside. The stars in the sky helped a bit, but she was definitely mindful of the fact that seeing even her feet was a challenge at this hour.

"You'll see."

Nicolás Farrell always seemed to have a taste for the dramatic. Artists, right? It didn't matter to Marla. She was happy to have him in her life, and aside from his requisite time alone, you know, to brood, and paint, and what have you, he was rarely unavailable to her. Everything she had waited for in her life was beginning to come together.

"Alright, Marla, hold steady."
"Okay."

Nic took her hand and helped her up the final crest of the hill, and there, below, resting on the beach, were two hundred lit tea candles, arranged to write the question, "Marla, will you marry me?"

*   *   *

"Daibh, my boy, sit down with me fer a while."

"Okay."

Pádraig had been bedridden for several days and had barely seen his grandson.

"Tell me what ya feel."

"Pardon?"

With a sigh, Pádraig pointed to his heart and repeated his request.

"Tell me what ya feel. Right now."

Daibhead had slowly become more used to the sober conversation the dying patrician evoked, atypical to what he remembered of him from before.

"Right now, I'm feelin' confused, Grampa. Confused."

Pádraig hummed in agreement.

"I'm not likin'- I'm not likin' this. This whole situation here, where I have ta come home an' see ya like this. It's not right."

"It's okay, Daibh. Keep talkin'."

"I keep hearin' how much worse yer body is gettin'. I can see that. I can see how pale ya look. I can see how small ya seem. It wasn't that long ago that I thought ya were the biggest man I ever knew. An' now, look, yer jus' this ol' man lyin' here, covered in a knit blanket."

"I am."

"But, you've never seemed more at peace, more in-tune with,

well, with everyt'in'."

Daibhead looked at Pádraig lying in the bed and saw a small glimmer of light flash across the elder man's eyes.

"How? How can ya be this way?"

"Daibhead, I don't have any special secret. There's not'in' magical about an old man, lyin' 'round all day, havin' a few moments of contemplation. I'd be out playin' football if my body would allow."

He laughed, a little, before it turned into a cough. After settling down again, he continued.

"The truth is, Daibh, that life is a continual struggle from the moment ya break free from the womb, until they start diggin' yer plot. I've lived a blessed life. Not a perfect one, no, certainly not. There are many t'ings I wished I could have accomplished that will never be crossed off my list, an' that's okay, I s'pose. They weren't meant ta be. They were dreams. They were idealistic, too good ta be true. Life isn't filled with that. It isn't meant ta be. It's about pushin' forward even though every t'ing ya thought ya wanted may never be. But I've been blessed. When ya never get anyt'in' perfect, ya begin ta learn ta see beauty in the imperfect. It's not settlin', naw, it's 'bout puttin' t'ings in perspective."

"I see."

"I hope ya do. I need ya to. I need ya ta promise me ya will."

*   *   *

"Take care of yourself, Alan."

Saraid was leaving for the night and said the words with the kind of casual emphasis to be expected. She had no idea of the weight he was carrying with him.

*   *   *

And, when I look up,
The stars don't say a thing
Back down on me,
So I lean up against you
And call you brother,
And, you call me brother, too,
While at the same time
You could just as easily stab me
And leave your brother there,
Under the stars

And our trust, brother,
Is that we don't,
That we continue not to,
For as long as we both can,
Until the sun shines
And it's not dark,
And I need not lean against you
Any longer in fear

36.
what me, think?

"He should have a strong name."

"He? What makes ya t'ink it'll be a boy, then, Sorley?"

"Yer right, Moira, there is a small chance it might be a girl. We should prolly have a backup plan."

"Backup plan? Sorley, there is a fifty percent chance that our child will be a girl. The least ya can do is come up with an equal list'f names for both."

Sorley looked at Moira with the look of a man who hadn't considered the possibility that he could produce anything other than a smaller version of himself. The thought of a baby girl, his girl, astounded him.

"I will. I'll t'ink of some great names for both."

*　　*　　*

"Get up, ya drunken bastard."

Fintan opened his eyes to see the scowling face of Sergei Abramov.

"Hallo, Serge. Y'alright?"

"I am not alright, Fintan, you're lying in front of my storefront, blocking me from getting in to start the day."

"It's rather early ta get a start on, Serge, I t'ink I'll sleep in a bit."

"You think you're funny, Fintan? You think that this is funny? I should call for the Gardaí, you must be good friends with them by now, no?"

"Shuddup, Serge. I'll jus' lay here fer a few more minutes, jus' till I wake up."

Fintan moved over slightly to allow Sergei to enter his shop. His eyes shut for what felt like a second when his body was jolted by the impact of a straw broom across his side.

"Get up, and go away, Fintan, before I call the Gardaí!"

It only took a second blow from Sergei's broom before Fin scooted off of the shop step and headed down the road.

"Fuck off, Serge."

Fin grumbled to himself for the entirety of his short walk home and then quickly crawled into his bed and shut his eyes to reclaim the sleep he had lost at the hands of his aggressor.

*　　*　　*

Words escape me,
I cannot hold them
Any longer,
They break me

I'm just a beggar man,
Beggin' for something
Beyond, beyond
This place

Do you trust me?

Every single sound
Slithers straight from my tongue
Every single sound
Without a fight

Do you trust me?

Would you love me

If you heard me
Say those things
I've long held dear?

Would you love me
If I whispered
A perfect poison
Right into your ear?

Every single sound
Slithers straight from my tongue
And you, you'll trust me
With every word

*   *   *

Niall the Chemist pulled out his set, set it upon the kitchen table, admired its beauty and began to disappear. There was no creation that afternoon, just a man lost in his chemicals. Dugan would transcend this world and nothing was certain beyond the black cloud.

37.
one step away from six feet deep

And we'll all just cry for something
That seems close enough to that.
Anything, anything at all
That seems close.
For, by now, we've given up
On hope and perfection,
Ideals, and forms.

We've seen no love,
No glory,
No peace,
No beauty,
But by God,
If we still believe,
There ought to be
Something like ideal
Out there, for me.

Yes, yes, of course,
Something like love,
That she might love me,
Enough, like that.

Yes, something like glory,
That it might be enough
To fill me,
To please me.

Something like peace,
The quiet between the cannons.

Something like beauty,
In all frailty,
To fill our eyes.

And when the night comes,
And it always does,
There might be something like rest,
Before tomorrow.

*   *   *

Pádraig's eyes closed. Eoghan stroked his father's hand as tears fell from his eyes.

*   *   *

Just a few miles down the road, in a small shed behind an old farmhouse lay Alan Brennan. He wouldn't be discovered for almost a week. When his body was found, only a couple discreet sentences were spoken, and a small obituary, less than fifty words occupied the local paper.

It wasn't for lack of words, or feelings that Alan's death barely registered, but for fear. Fear to admit the unthinkable, that his tragic life and death was the rule and not the exception. Fear to admit his weakness, his cross to bear, was not his alone, but that it was ours as a whole. When he ached for acceptance, he felt the longing that we all feel when we're not quite right. When he cried, his tears were oceans of pain. When he questioned his place on this earth, he asked for all of us. When he begged God for forgiveness, he spoke the words we were too proud to mouth. And then, when he could carry the burden no longer, fear that we would follow.

38.
return to the train station

Daniél carried the luggage, while Saraid walked beside him, her face wearing a light smile, uncommon for this early hour.

The crisp morning air hit their faces as they stepped onto the platform. Years of waiting, a life unfulfilled, now lay behind them. At this moment the past ended and the present was waning, leading into a newborn future for them, carte blanche.

The sound of the approaching train gave everyone on the platform a jolt of energy, alertness, and a touch of nervousness. Anticipation was contagious, each person double-checking their pockets for tickets they knew to be present a thousand times before.

Danny read his ticket with surreal belief, stroking the paper to affirm its reality. Today he leaves. Beside him stood Sara, the love of his life. Her hand held a ticket identical to his, with the minor exception of seat number, bound for the same journey. They were destined to travel together.

His heart beat with a healthy rhythm, for what seemed like the first time, ever. The lethargy of his trough period long gone, the hyperactive pulsations of the early summer now settled, Danny's heart was finally beating as it should.

Sara's stomach was another story, as butterflies danced about. She watched Doyle with admiration and saw his beauty shining through; the dark thunderous clouds that had circled him for so long had dissipated. Here, in front of her, was a true man, filled with every trait she could ever want, beyond what she could ever need. She will never let him go, again. How funny it is that the heart can easily recognise this, before we ever do, and it takes trials in life, numerous detours before we wander back to the place we were always meant to be.

He looked up from the ticket he had confirmed to be real and saw her watching him, her faint morning smile radiating warmth that only he could feel. Gorgeous, he thought, she was absolutely gorgeous, without compare. I'm not just an exaggerating fool, love, to tell you this. Anyone who was there could see; these two lovers were bound for the stars. Poets can take liberty on occasion to gloss over the details, but on that early August morning, I tell you the truth, I saw the closest thing to love that I do believe I'll ever see.

Daniél Doyle took Saraid Doran's face in his hands, brushed her hair back, leaned in, and whispered in her ear. Her eyes welt up, and tears flowed down her cheeks. He pulled back, and entered the carriage car.

*   *   *

Daibhead Shannon sat on a bench, watching the horizon, waiting; wondering what the next locomotive would bring.

epilogue

It's been a long night. I really ought to be heading out, but it was kind of you to entertain my tales, Molly. I didn't know what to expect from you, but it's clear that you still have a small amount of patience for me and my ramblings.

I hope your boy and you find yourself at something like peace. I know it's hard, believe me, I know. But the whiskey and my dreams keep me content until the next day breaks. I should hope for nothing less for you. If we still know the same Lord, I think we'll agree that He gives us always just a bit more than we can handle, but we manage nonetheless, am I right? Why should now be any different?

Now. Now, tonight. I waited for this night, I really did, Molly. I waited for the chance to tell you everything and I guess I went about it in a really roundabout way, but I think I told you what I needed to say. Almost everything, that is. I forgot to tell you what Daniél Doyle said to Saraid Doran. What made her eyes fill with tears on that platform. Lean close to me, I won't touch your face, I couldn't try even if I had more courage or spirits in me, but lean close, and I'll whisper it to you. He held her face, Molly, and he brushed her hair out of the way, pulling himself close, and whispered to her:

"You'll never have to travel alone again."

Do you know why he said that? No, wait, of course not, you couldn't. It wasn't part of the story, it didn't happen over that summer, but a few years before our story began. I wish I had said it earlier. To think I've been waiting for such a long time and then to mess up the dramatic ending! Two years prior to the beginning of our tale, Saraid told Daniél why she had to leave:

"I have to go, Daniél, because standing still is taking me nowhere. The world keeps spinning, drawing us into the night, disappearing over the horizon. And yet you stand still, and just let the orbit's inertia pull you into tomorrow, and the next, without a fight. I can't. I have to go, I

have to be in today, on my terms, in my own control. Perhaps, one day, as the world spins, and our orbits align, you'll step forward and meet me there. Until then, I'll travel, because waiting just isn't for me."

gratitude

Much thanks and love goes out to all the amazing friends that have stuck with me through stormy patches and continue to stick it out.

Thanks to all the creative brothers and sisters I've met along the way that have challenged me to pursue my art.

Thanks to my parents for being consistently supportive and understanding. I am who I am because of you.

Much love to my sister and my grandparents for being my biggest fans. I apologise for the naughty words I use in this book.

Most of all, thank you for holding this book in your hands; it means the world to me that you're reading something that I poured my heart and soul into. Without you, the reader, all these words are just crazy thoughts trapped in one man's head.

about the author

Brent Stephen Smith was born in Calgary, Alberta in 1985. He holds a B.A. (Hons.) from Bishop's University and a M.A. from Simon Fraser University. He currently lives in Ottawa, Ontario, though he still claims White Rock, B.C. as his hometown.

Something Like Ideal is his first novel.